TRUST IN ME

When Kerra Morrison is named main beneficiary in her uncle's will, her cousins Sarah and David are furious their father favoured her over them. So when someone attempts to sabotage Kerra's new tearoom, her cousins seem to be the obvious culprits. But are there darker forces at work? The town's GP, Dr Duncan Crombie, comes to her aid. It would be easy to fall for such a man — if he didn't keep throwing up barriers every time they seem to be getting close . . .

Books by Rena George
in the Linford Romance Library:

DANGER AT MELLIN COVE
ANOTHER CHANCE

RENA GEORGE

TRUST IN ME

Complete and Unabridged

LINFORD
Leicester

First published in Great Britain

First Linford Edition
published 2013

A catalogue record for this book is available
from the British Library.

ISBN 978–1–4448–1756–0

Published by
F. A. Thorpe (Publishing)
Anstey, Leicestershire

Set by Words & Graphics Ltd.
Anstey, Leicestershire
Printed and bound in Great Britain by
T. J. International Ltd., Padstow, Cornwall

This book is printed on acid-free paper

Endless Possibilities

Matthew West cleared his throat, adjusted his rimless spectacles and straightened the documents in front of him before glancing at the tense faces gathered around his desk. It was the reading of the late Sinclair Morrison's will, and there was sure to be a ruckus. He knew most of the people seated in his tiny office and nodded to the deceased's younger brother, Fraser, and his wife, Rosemary. Sinclair's son, David, had fixed him with an irritated stare, while his sibling, Sarah, looked impatient.

The two other young women in the room were strangers to Matthew. His eyes settled on the one he was sure was Kerra Morrison. He knew from Sinclair's description that she was pretty if she smiled, but this morning the huge blue eyes were clouded. She pushed back a fringe of corn-coloured hair as she glanced around her companions.

'Well, you all know why we are here, so I won't beat about the bush,' he began.

Kerra shifted uneasily in her chair. She'd never before been a beneficiary in anyone's will. To her mind the whole thing was happening with unseemly speed. It was less than a week since they'd all stood in the tiny churchyard in Craigallen — in her case, blinking back tears — as the minister spoke the appropriate words over her uncle Sinclair's grave. The plaintive notes of 'Flowers Of The Forest' still rang in her ears, and she remembered the piper's slow, respectful strides as he moved away from the assembled mourners, his music fading as he went. Kerra thought it was the most moving thing she'd ever witnessed.

Now, here they all were again, gathered in the solicitor's office, awaiting the details of his will. She glanced across at her mum and dad; they looked as uncomfortable as she felt. She caught their eyes and gave them a reassuring smile. Her cousins, Sarah and David, sat opposite. There was a glitter of excitement in their eyes as they watched the solicitor straighten his papers for the umpteenth time.

Why didn't the man just get on with it, David thought irritably. Since his uncle and aunt, and young cousin, Kerra, were here, the old man had obviously left them small bequests. His gaze fixed on the woman sitting next to Kerra. Why was she here? She was his father's shop assistant — surely he hadn't left her any money?

Fiona Crombie caught his glare and felt her face flush. She'd no idea why she was here, but the sooner the whole business was over with the sooner she could get back to the shop. She'd put up a notice on the door explaining the closure, but now she was wondering if she'd been summoned here to be told to lock up the shop for good.

No-one in the family had ever

appeared interested in following in old Mr Morrison's footsteps. David had his own garage business which, judging by the number of times he appeared at the shop and clattered down the metal spiral staircase to his father's workshop for yet another heated demand for cash, seemed to be in constant financial trouble. His younger sister, Sarah, had married a bank manager and had three children at fee-paying schools in Aberdeen. Fiona suspected they were living above their means in their big house here in Inverness.

As they waited for the solicitor to continue, Kerra's eyes scanned the room, taking in the enormous mahogany glass-fronted bookcase, with its leather-bound volumes of legal books, and the bundles of files on his desk.

The place hadn't been as easy to find as she'd expected. She'd followed Matthew West's instructions to the letter, turning from one street in Inverness's busy shopping centre into another. But when she arrived at the

4

double-fronted office, she'd felt the first stabs of apprehension. She still couldn't believe her uncle had named her as a beneficiary, but then he had known how much she had admired the painting that hung in his draper's shop above his workroom. The artist wasn't well known, but he had captured the magic of the snow-capped peaks of the Cairngorms as they stretched up to an indigo sky. Kerra smiled to herself. Perhaps her uncle had left her the picture.

Reluctant to enter the office on her own, she looked up and down the street hoping to spot her parents' car. She checked her watch. She was 15 minutes early. She stood looking at the glass door, wondering if she should go inside when the decision was taken out of her hands. The door opened and a small, neat woman with permed brown hair and periwinkle blue eyes beckoned her.

'Are you here for reading of Mr Morrison's will, dear?'

Kerra nodded.

5

'Just follow me,' she said. 'Mr West is expecting you.'

Kerra followed the woman along a dark corridor with wooden doors to the left and right. She opened the one at the end and stepped back.

'This is — ' She turned to Kerra. 'I'm sorry. I didn't ask your name.'

Kerra opened her mouth to speak when a draught from the street door indicated that the others had arrived. They all trooped in, nodding to the solicitor and taking the seats he signalled they should occupy.

Matthew West lowered his spectacles, watching them as they settled.

'We'll have tea at the end,' he offered, his gaze resting on Kerra. 'I knew your uncle rather well,' he said. 'A great pity him going like that. Much too young.'

Kerra's uncle Sinclair had been seventy-six, but Mr West was right. He had been much too full of life to be struck down with pneumonia.

'I understand you visited him recently?'

Kerra smiled, remembering.

'That's right,' she said. Had it only been a few weeks ago? Marcus, proprietor of the Glasgow restaurant where she was assistant chef, had pleaded with her to come to his rescue by taking temporary charge of the kitchens in a wine bar he owned in Inverness. Someone had misjudged the holiday rota, which had left them short staffed.

The arrangement suited Kerra very well for it meant she could go home to Craigallen every night, where her parents ran a smallholding. And since the wine bar was only a few streets away from her uncle's shop, she could visit him regularly. When Fiona, Sinclair's only member of staff, came down with flu and he'd been about to close the draper's shop for the week, Kerra had stepped into the breach, explaining she was free during the day. It had been exhausting, because she'd been working late hours in the wine bar kitchen, but she couldn't let her uncle down.

Mr West was nodding.

'He told me about that.'

It had been no imposition to work in the shop that week. She had really enjoyed it. It was certainly different from the hectic, steamy kitchens she was used to. The pace of life in a country draper's shop was more sedate. Every time the door tinkled she looked up expectantly, happy at the arrival of a potential customer. Most of them were older women who preferred the kind of traditional fabrics the shop stocked. Occasionally the tinkle announced a male customer, calling to enquire if his suit was ready for collection, or to be measured up for a new one. But the tall, broad-shouldered man with the earnest grey eyes and sandy hair didn't fit any of these patterns. With his athletic build and deep mahogany tan, Kerra thought he would be more at home on some expensive foreign holiday beach than the streets of Inverness. But the green tweed jacket he wore was appropriate enough for these parts.

The stranger's brow furrowed and he looked perplexed when he saw Kerra behind the counter.

'I was looking for Fiona,' he said, glancing about him as though he expected to find her in one of the shop corners. His eyes flicked up to the clock. 'She doesn't usually go out at lunchtime.'

Annoyed at his accusing tone, Kerra spoke crisply.

'She's not here today.' She was beginning to feel uncomfortable under his appraising stare and wondered how much of Fiona's business she should tell this man.

'So where is she?' he continued, holding her gaze.

'She's having some time off. I'm standing in for her.'

His eyebrows shot up.

'Well, I can see that, but why is she taking time off? It's not like her.' He suddenly looked anxious. 'There's nothing wrong with her, is there?'

Kerra cleared her throat. She'd no

idea why she was being so cagey with him. He obviously knew Fiona well, and she had to admit he seemed genuinely concerned.

'Fiona has flu. I'm helping out while she's away.'

His face creased into a worried frown.

'Why didn't you say so? I'd better call in and see her.'

He turned to leave the shop, but she called after him, 'Surely it would be better to ring first?'

The stranger looked round, the merest hint of a smile touching his lips.

'Fiona won't mind,' he called back.

Kerra watched him cross the road and get into a little red sports car. She pursed her lips thoughtfully. Fiona had kept quiet about him. He obviously knew her well. He didn't look like he would be the girl's type, but then . . . She could feel an uncomfortable little stab of emotion deep inside her, but she refused to admit it could be jealousy. It was definitely not that.

Mr West's lilting Highland voice brought her back to the present. He was nodding.

'Your uncle told me how you stepped into the breach when Miss Crombie here was ill.'

Her cousin, David, gave an irritated cough.

'Can we get on?' he said sharply. 'I have places to be.'

The solicitor sighed, placed a finger on his spectacles and pushed them back up his nose. Out of the corner of her eye Kerra registered the impatient glance that passed between Sarah and David.

'Right, let's get started,' Mr West said.

He began by outlining a number of bequests. Sarah and David were each to receive £15,000, with smaller amounts to be placed in trust funds for Sarah's three children and David's two youngsters. Another £10,000 had been left to Kerra, and each of her parents. Kerra started. Had she heard that right? Had her uncle Sinclair really left her £10,000? Her hand flew to her mouth and her mother turned, smiling, to touch her daughter's hand. Across the room she could see Sarah and David staring at her. There was no mistaking their disapproving glares.

Mr West hadn't finished.

'Mr Morrison has not forgotten you, Miss Crombie.'

Fiona looked up. Kerra could see that her hands were shaking. He read from the document.

'In recognition of her five years of loyal service, I bequeath five thousand pounds to Fiona Crombie.'

Fiona let out a little exclamation of delight.

'I don't know what to say,' she said, blushing.

The solicitor smiled and then his gaze swept the room.

'And now for the main part of the will.'

They all waited.

'The house known as Muirend, and

all of its contents, I bequeath to my daughter, Sarah, and my son, David, for them to dispose of as they choose. The proceeds to be split evenly between them.'

Sarah frowned, confused.

'Dad's left the house to both of us? I don't understand. He always said the house would be mine. David was to get the business. This isn't fair.'

'I drew this will up for your father six months ago, Mrs Gillan. I can assure you that these are your father's wishes.'

Sarah's eyes flew wide.

'Six months ago!' She was out of her chair. 'You mean my father changed it?'

Mr West cleared his throat again.

'If I might be permitted to continue?'

An uneasy feeling was beginning to creep into Kerra's bones. There had been an extra twinkle in her old uncle's eyes the last time she saw him. Was this what he'd been planning? She glanced across at her cousins' anxious faces and her brow furrowed.

'Well, go on,' David urged. This was

beginning to look good for him. If he was to get the business and half the proceeds from the sale of the house it would not only dig him out of his current financial hole, but it would set him up nicely for the future. Then a thought struck him and he sprang forward in his chair. 'Surely he's not making us share the business as well?'

The solicitor's eyes narrowed.

'No, Mr Morrison,' he said curtly. 'The business is not to be split.' He looked up and met Kerra's eyes before quoting from the document. 'The shop and work premises in Lewis Street, Inverness, together with all the stock therein and the goodwill that I have built up over the years, I leave to my niece, Kerra Morrison, who has been more of a daughter to me than my own children. She's shown me love and compassion with no sign of the greed I see in the eyes of my son David and daughter Sarah.'

Kerra froze. The reactions of everyone around her seemed to be playing out in slow motion. They all turned to her, wide-eyed. Then her cousins were out of their chairs.

'What does he mean she's more of a daughter than me?' Sarah barked, looking wildly round the room. 'This is outrageous!' She turned on Kerra, jabbing a finger at her. 'This is all your doing.'

David put a restraining hand on his sister's arm, his face white with shock and fury as he fought to control his voice. He turned to Matthew West.

'You've made a mistake, sir.' He spat out the words. 'My father could be a cantankerous old devil sometimes, but he'd never do something like this to us. The house was always to be hers, and the business was to come to me.' His eyes bulged with rage.

Mr West pursed his lips.

'This is a legal document, Mr Morrison. These were your father's wishes.'

Kerra was trembling. She hadn't asked for this. The last thing she wanted was to take her cousins' inheritance. Through no fault of hers she'd been thrown into the middle of what was now certain to be a horrendous family feud.

'Are you absolutely sure this is what Uncle Sinclair wanted, Mr West?' she asked meekly.

He tapped the papers.

'It's all here in black and white, my dear.'

Kerra's dad was now also on his feet.

'Whatever else my brother was, he was never a fool. And if he wanted you to have his business, Kerra, then he knew what he was doing.'

Kerra was shaking her head, still trying to take it all in.

Fiona touched her arm and whispered in her ear.

'Congratulations, Kerra. You deserve this.'

David was leaning menacingly across Mr West's desk.

'We're not leaving it like this.'

'Too right,' Sarah growled behind

him. 'We'll contest the will.'

Mr West had eased himself out of his chair and put out a restraining hand.

'If everyone can just calm down and allow me to finish.'

'There's more?' David demanded.

'There's more,' the solicitor said, waving the angry pair back to their seats. 'Mr Morrison has added a codicil.' He glanced down at the papers. 'It's this,' he said. 'If any of the beneficiaries contest the will, their legacies will be forfeited and divided up and distributed amongst the charities previously nominated by me.'

David and Sarah stared at him, then at each other. David took his sister's arm and yanked her from her chair, pushing her towards the door. Then he turned and glared back at Kerra.

'You haven't heard the end of this. So don't start congratulating yourself just yet.'

Kerra shuddered as the door slammed shut behind them. For a moment no-one spoke, then Mr West extracted a white handkerchief from his pocket and mopped his brow.

'That was unfortunate,' he said quietly. 'Don't let it daunt you. Your uncle was my friend as well as my client, and I know that he wanted you to have his business.'

'But I don't know a thing about running a draper's shop, let alone anything about gents' outfitting.'

The solicitor smiled.

'Your uncle has given you a very desirable property in the centre of Inverness.' He smiled. 'The possibilities are endless. It's up to you what you do with it.'

A Business Proposition

'The solicitor was right,' Fraser Morrison said as Kerra sat opposite her parents in a little restaurant near the solicitor's office.

'I can't get my head round this, Dad. I mean, why me?'

Rosemary Morrison patted her daughter's hand.

'Because you were more like a daughter to him than Sarah ever was, and as for David — ' Her face twisted into a grimace. 'That pair lived only a few miles from their father yet they never visited him. Well, no, let me correct that. They did go to see him, but only when they wanted something — and that was usually money.'

'Oh, Mum, they weren't that bad.'

'Your mother's right, Kerra. Sinclair said as much to me. They were always on the scrounge. Sarah's three are all at fee-paying schools, and then there's that big house of theirs to keep up. That won't come cheap. Ivan may be a bank manager, but I'd be surprised if he earned enough to justify the kind of lifestyle they seem to enjoy.'

Rosemary shook her head.

'It's the children I feel sorry for.'

'Thanks, Mum. I feel worse than ever now. It sounds to me as though Sarah and Ivan needed that inheritance.'

Rosemary tutted.

'Not needed, Kerra — just wanted it. Don't even think of feeling sorry for them. Sarah and David can sell the house at Muirend. They won't go short.'

'But they were expecting to get the lot,' Kerra reminded them bleakly. Then a thought struck her. 'You don't suppose David's garage is in trouble, and that's the reason he reacted the way he did?'

'I wouldn't be surprised,' Fraser said. 'David never was much of a business-man. Too busy chasing the girls for that.

You'd think that with a broken marriage behind him he would have learned his lesson.'

'Let's not feel too sorry for them,' Rosemary cut in. 'It's not as though their father didn't look after them.'

Kerra knew her parents were right, but it didn't stop her feeling guilty. She'd never forget that look of loathing on her cousins' faces as they slammed out of the solicitor's office. She'd made two powerful enemies today.

Kerra lay awake for most of the night. It was unbearable to think that Sarah and David might hate her. Her parents could be right, of course, and Uncle Sinclair really had wanted her to have the business. Even his solicitor had said so — and she trusted Matthew West. Still, it wasn't something that rested easily with her. But on the other hand Kerra thought of all the things she could do with the proceeds of the sale.

It was a prime site property, Mr West had said. She'd have to get a valuation, but from what she'd been told there would be more than enough to set her dreams in motion. She sat up in the darkness. The idea came to her in a blinding light. The solution was so obvious. She was annoyed she hadn't thought of it immediately.

★ ★ ★

Matthew West slid his spectacles up his nose in the now-familiar gesture and studied Kerra.

'Are you sure you know what you're doing?'

She smiled.

'I've given it a lot of thought. Sarah and David may have blotted their copybooks with their father, but I don't see why their children should suffer. They are my second cousins, after all.' She paused, choosing her words carefully. 'I want Sarah's three children and David's two little ones to each have five per cent of the proceeds from the sale of the business. The money will obviously need to be put into trust funds for them until they are of age, but I'll take your advice about that.'

The solicitor scrunched his eyebrows together, and Kerra smiled at the look of uncertainty on his round face.

'There's one more thing,' she said. 'I want you to put the property on the market straight away.'

It was a full minute before Matthew West spoke. He took the time to compose himself, compressed his lips tightly together as he considered the implications of what he'd just heard. Then he looked up, his eyes meeting hers.

'Your uncle was right. You are an extraordinary young woman, Kerra. I can see why Sinclair put so much trust in you.' His mouth curved into a smile and he shrugged. 'Who knows? Maybe he even foresaw this outcome.'

Kerra smiled back at him.

'Maybe he did, Mr West.'

'Even so.' The blue eyes were studying her again. 'I still advise caution. What you are suggesting would mean you would be relinquishing a quarter of your inheritance. That's a very big step to take and I would be remiss in my duty if I didn't advise caution.'

Kerra opened her mouth to speak, but he put up a hand.

'You shouldn't make any definite decisions until you've considered all the possibilities.'

'I'm really grateful for all your advice, and I know that you have my interests at heart, but my mind is made up.'

The solicitor struggled out of his chair and came round to shake her hand.

'I still think you should wait a week or two.' The rimless glasses slid back down his nose and he left them there, surveying his young client from over the top of them.

But Kerra shook her head.

'I'm quite clear about what I want to do, and I want you to sell Uncle Sinclair's business.'

'Well, at least I agree with that

decision, but selling businesses takes time.'

'I wasn't expecting you to sell it as a going concern. I can't see too many prospective buyers wanting to run an old-fashioned tailoring business.' She gave a wistful smile. 'There's not many craftsmen of my uncle's calibre left. No, please just put the basic property on the market. If it sells as a going concern then that will be a bonus.'

Mr West gave a deep sigh.

'Well, if you're sure that's what you want, then I'll get on to it immediately. It should get a good price. You'll be a wealthy woman, Kerra.' He frowned. 'Or you would be if you weren't so set on giving so much of it away.'

She raised an eyebrow, letting the man know the issue was not up for further discussion.

'OK,' he said, putting up a hand. 'I'll put the wheels in motion for the property to go on the market today.'

Kerra took his hand again and shook it, smiling.

'I know the arrangements will be in good hands.'

Matthew West stared at the door for some time after it closed behind Kerra, and his pursed lips twitched into a smile. He nodded to himself. He was going to like young Kerra Morrison.

* * *

The bell gave its familiar tinkle as Kerra went in to her uncle's shop. Fiona smiled when she recognised the newcomer. It transformed her face, and Kerra realised with surprise just how pretty the girl was. Her blonde hair was long, but while Kerra's was straight, Fiona's was a mass of springy curls, which today she was keeping in check with a black ribbon, tied back on the nape of her neck. The bright green top she wore made her light blue eyes seem almost turquoise. No wonder the good-looking young man who'd come searching for her that day had fallen for her. She felt a little stab of envy.

'Hello, Kerra. You're bright and early. I take it you've come to look over your new business?'

Kerra looked up quickly, searching her face for any sign of bitterness, but found none.

'I've come to see you, actually, Fiona. There are things we need to discuss.'

Fiona spread her arms to the empty shop.

'Well, as you can see, I'm not exactly rushed off my feet at the moment. Shall I put the kettle on?'

'No, I've got a better idea.' Kerra grinned. 'I'll put the kettle on. Tea or coffee?' she called back over her shoulder as she went through to the back shop. She emerged five minutes later with two mugs and a plate of biscuits on a tray. There was still no sign of any customers.

Fiona took a sip her coffee.

'If I'm speaking out of turn just tell me, but you didn't deserve the way your cousins behaved towards you yesterday, Kerra. Your uncle thought the world of you.' She frowned as she stared into her mug. 'I'm sure he knew exactly what he was doing. Sarah and David were always upsetting him, not that he said a word against them to me, but I could see the sadness in his eyes after their visits.'

'They used to come to the shop?' Kerra couldn't keep the surprise out of her voice.

Fiona nodded, and inclined her head in the direction of the door that led down to Sinclair's workroom.

'They did when they were looking for something, and it was usually money.' Her face took on a grim smile. 'Your cousin, David, was a regular visitor.'

Kerra felt irritated. Fiona meant no harm, but she didn't want to hear any more of this. She took a deep breath.

'You must be curious about why I'm here.'

If the sudden change of subject surprised Fiona, she didn't show it.

'I've been making plans,' Kerra said, picking up her coffee and warming her hands around the mug. 'I've decided to sell this place.'

Fiona nodded, her expression serious.

'That's what I expected. I couldn't see you wanting to run a business like this. It'll be a bit of a wrench, though. I've worked for your uncle since I left school.'

'How do you feel about working for me now, Fiona?'

The girl stared at her.

'I thought you just said — '

'I mean in my new business.' She watched Fiona's eyebrows shoot up and grinned. 'I'm going to open a tearoom in Craigallen, and I want you to run it for me.'

'Me? Run a tearoom?' She got up and ran to hug Kerra. 'I can't imagine anything I'd love more.'

'Well, there's a bit more to it than that.' Kerra laughed, disentangling herself. 'I'll need to find premises that are big enough for my outside catering.'

Fiona's mouth dropped open.

'Don't look so surprised. I'm a chef, remember?'

Fiona nodded. She was so full of questions she didn't know where to start, so she decided to listen to Kerra explaining things in her own way. When she'd finished, Fiona sat back.

'Wow! That's a fabulous idea, but will there be enough business for you in Craigallen?'

'I think so,' Kerra said. 'The town could do with a good tearoom. We could make the place really friendly, and serve home baking, and furnish it in a cosy, homely way.'

Fiona was nodding enthusiastically.

'As far as the outside catering goes, we could build up a good business locally. We could provide the food at local events and functions, children's birthday parties. We could provide a meal delivery service to people's homes.' Kerra's eyes shone. 'What do you think?'

'I think it's wonderful. Just tell me how I can help.'

Kerra put down her empty mug.

'It will be quicker to sell the property if it's not a going business concern. So I might need to sell the stock.'

'Maybe I could help,' Fiona offered. 'Mr Morrison trusted me to deal with the firms that supplied his stock, so I have all the contacts.' She looked up shyly. 'Of course, there's always my little inheritance. It's only that five thousand pounds your uncle left me, but I'd be happy to invest it in the new business, if you need it.'

Kerra smiled.

'I don't think that will be necessary, Fiona, but I appreciate the offer. If you could just check out the possibility of selling that stock then that would be a great help.' Her mind was racing ahead. 'I noticed while I've been home that McAlpine's in the High Street in Craigallen had a closing-down notice in the window.'

'That's right,' Fiona said enthusiastically. 'But it's not been McAlpine's for some time, though I think they still own the premises and rent it out. The present occupiers are fairly new to the area.' She shook her head. 'Can't imagine why they thought a trendy fashion shop would be a success in a farming area like Craigallen.'

'I'll call in on them this afternoon,' Kerra said, feeling a surge of excitement.

The shop door tinkled and they both looked up and smiled at the first customer of the day. Kerra slipped off her stool, collected their mugs, and took the tray through the back before leaving.

The road outside was busier than when she'd arrived and she took time to look around her. She took in the busy bookshop and newsagent's next door, then there was the butcher's shop, where the tourists flocked to purchase haggis. The Crown Hotel was on the corner, and the railway station at the end of the road. Her heart gave a little flip. Matthew West was right; Uncle Sinclair's property was a very desirable package for someone.

Her mind was on her future plans as she stepped off the pavement. She didn't see the white van sweeping past and would have walked in front of it if a hand hadn't grabbed her and pulled her back. She swung round, shaken, and found herself looking into a pair of familiar grey eyes.

'You could have killed yourself! What were you thinking, wandering out into the road like that?' he demanded angrily.

Kerra shook her arm free from his grip and glared up at the man who'd come into her uncle's shop looking for Fiona. He'd been right, of course, she could have been killed. She should have been grateful to him for saving her, but the fact that he was now chastising her as though she was a naughty child made her blood boil.

'I'm very grateful to you,' she said stiffly. 'But I am capable of taking care of myself.'

His eyebrows drew up into a frown.

'It didn't seem like it from where I was standing. Wait a minute . . . haven't we met before?'

'I shouldn't think so,' Kerra lied, glancing both ways to make sure there was no danger this time of colliding with any passing traffic.

'I'm sure we have,' he called after her as she hurried away from him.

Her heart was thudding and she was shaking, but she wasn't sure if that was because she had almost ended up under the wheels of a van, or because she was now in the debt of this very arrogant, handsome man.

The Crofters' Arms

Back in her car Kerra took deep breaths. The incident had shaken her. The man had obviously been on his way to see Fiona and no doubt he would be telling her about the silly woman he'd just been forced to rescue. She waited until the hammering of her heart had stilled before switching on the engine and joining the city traffic.

It was a 30-minute drive along the loch road to Craigallen. Once she was through the busy city centre she relaxed, enjoying the incredible views of sparking water and purple hills that every new twist of the road brought.

Her family's smallholding was a mile on the other side of Craigallen, and she slowed as she drove along the High Street, keen to get another look at the double-fronted shop she was now certain she wanted to buy.

Excitement swept through her. She was already planning how the place would look when it was the Craigallen tearoom. All her dreams were coming together. This was the business she had always wanted, but to be able to do it in her home town, with her family and friends all around her . . . well, it didn't get much better than that.

'Thank you, Uncle Sinclair,' she whispered to herself, and a tear rolled down her cheek.

But she was smiling again when she drove up the lane to the croft house where she'd grown up. She saw the curtains twitch at the kitchen window, and her mother waving through the glass. Her parents were at the table when she got in, a bowl of home-made broth in front of each of them.

'I wasn't sure if you'd be back for lunch,' Rosemary Morrison said, looking up as her daughter walked in. 'But there's plenty more in the pot. Help yourself, Kerra, love.'

She did, accepting the slice of crusty

bread her father cut for her. The soup was delicious, as she knew it would be. She was in no doubt from whom she had inherited her culinary talents.

Fraser Morrison pushed his empty bowl away and sat back, meeting his daughter's excited eyes.

'OK. We can see you're bursting to tell us something.'

Kerra took a deep breath and related the events of the morning, leaving out the instructions she had given her solicitor to set up trusts for her cousins.

'Well, you've been busy,' Fraser said, looking at his wife.

Kerra's mother was biting her lip, her eyes troubled.

'A catering business,' she repeated uncertainly. 'Are you sure? It's a huge commitment to take on, I mean, how do you know people here will want it?' She'd been stacking their bowls in the sink and was now rattling out mugs and tea things. 'And a tearoom? They've got a café in Craigallen. You'd be taking away Mr Rossi's business.'

'It's a completely different thing, Mum,' Kerra reasoned. 'He sells ice-cream and sweets. Besides, he's only got two tables. The kind of tearoom I'm planning will sell home-made cakes, scones, sandwiches. It'll be a place where the locals can meet for a natter over a cup of tea when they're shopping.'

'What about the catering thing, love? How will that work?' her father asked.

'Well, it's obviously something I'll have to build up, but I know I can do it.'

She outlined all the ideas she had previously discussed with Fiona, and her parents exchanged a look. Her father pursed his lips and scratched his head.

'I can't see Murray Glenn being happy about that. You know the Crofters' Arms provides most of the outside catering around here.'

'It's all healthy competition, Dad,' Kerra cut in, her eyes shining. She didn't know Mr Glenn. He'd bought

Craigallen's only hotel a year earlier and, from what she'd heard, he wasn't popular. It had always been a friendly place, and with its snug bar tucked away as it was, it was frequented by most of the men in town. But after its renovation the new owner made it clear that he didn't want people in working clothes in his new bar. He was concentrating on attracting customers from further afield. If Murray Glenn didn't like what she was planning to do then he would have to lump it.

'Actually, I was hoping to have a look round McAlpine's shop this afternoon. Any chance of you giving him a ring, Dad? You know him better than I do.'

Fraser nodded.

'Jock won't mind that, I'm sure, but he'll have to check with the couple who lease it from him.'

'Terrible shame that fashion shop having to close.' Rosemary shook her head. 'Rory and Daisy Forsyth are such a nice couple, but they need to be in a bigger town to sell hats and dresses like that.'

Fraser had gone into the hall to the phone and Kerra could hear him talking to Jock McAlpine.

'Thanks, Jock. Three o'clock it is, then. I'll tell Kerra.'

He came back into the kitchen and nodded.

'You hear that?'

Kerra rushed forward to hug him.

'Thanks, Dad. You're an angel.'

McAlpine's had been a hardware store for as long as Kerra could remember, but when ill health forced Jock McAlpine to retire he couldn't find a buyer. There were two huge DIY stores in the retail estate just outside Inverness, and these days everybody took their business there. So with a heavy heart, Jock had had to find tenants willing to lease the property.

The first couple had turned it into a grocery shop, but they hadn't lasted a year before they were forced out of business. It followed the same pattern for the current tenants, the Forsyths. They had the enthusiasm and, as far as he could see, neither of them was shy of hard work, but the customers just didn't come. Now here was Fraser Morrison's girl coming along with yet another idea for the shop. He was hoping for third time lucky.

Kerra arrived bang on time, and was relieved to see the Forsyths had been expecting her. They introduced themselves and they shook hands before Daisy disappeared through the back to make a pot of tea while Kerra and Rory waited in the main shop area for Jock to arrive.

'If you're local then you probably already know your way around the place,' Rory commented.

Kerra shook her head.

'I used to come with my dad when he needed spare parts for his farm machinery.' She looked round, remembering the earthy smells of the old ironmonger's shop. McAlpine's had carried an eclectic mix of stock, ranging from bags of seed potatoes to new pine posts, and from drawers of nails to rolls of thick plastic sheeting. The surroundings she now found herself in were all very feminine and pastel, with floaty dresses, summer hats, and a display of seasonally fashionable tops in an array of ice-cream colours. It looked and smelled nothing like the McAlpine's she remembered.

The front door opened with a flourish and Jock McAlpine strode in.

'Hope I haven't kept you waiting,' he said, his warm brown eyes crinkling into a welcome. He put a hand out to Kerra. 'I wouldn't have recognised you,' he said, smiling. 'You only reached Fraser's waist last time I saw you.'

Daisy arrived with her tray of mugs and they all took one as they discussed the layout of the premises.

The area at the front, with its two big windows on to the High Street, would be perfect for her tearoom. Kerra had never been behind the scenes in the shop and hadn't realised how much space there was through the back. A door led out to a car park at the rear of the building. It was perfect. She couldn't keep the smile from her face. Her catering business was going to work. She was sure of it.

Outside in the street she turned to look back at the shop front, imagining the changes she would make, when she felt strong hands grip her shoulders and a voice said, 'Don't you ever look where you're going?'

Kerra didn't have to spin round this time to identify the voice. She knew exactly who he was — or rather, she didn't, but he no longer seemed like a stranger. When she did spin to look at him, she expected to see an irritated scowl, but he was grinning at her, the grey eyes teasing.

'We do seem to make rather a habit of this,' he said.

Kerra narrowed her eyes.

'Are you stalking me?'

He threw back his head and laughed

so heartily that Kerra flushed with annoyance.

'I'm not stalking you, Miss Morrison,' he said at last. 'And before you ask, my sister told me who you are.'

Kerra's mouth dropped open.

'Fiona is your sister? Well, that explains a lot.'

He raised an eyebrow, but didn't pursue her comment.

'I feel I owe you an apology,' he said. 'I was a bit over-zealous in my comments about your . . . ' He gave her a slow grin that sent her pulses pounding ' . . . your jaywalking this morning.'

She was about to protest then decided against it. He had apologised, after all.

'I was wondering if I could make up for my lack of gallantry earlier by inviting you to dinner this evening?' He gestured in the direction of the Crofters' Arms. 'I'm told it's under new ownership.'

She tried not to show her surprise at

the unexpected invitation. Dinner with Fiona's brother might not be so bad, and besides, she would be able to get a look at the controversial Murray Glenn.

Kerra had often taken her parents to the Crofters' Arms for bar meals on her visits home. It had the relaxed, homely atmosphere that was often missing in Glasgow's trendy wine bars. But the first thing that struck her tonight as she walked into the bar was the stark unfamiliarity of the place. All the old ambience had gone.

The comfortable, mismatched furniture had been replaced by smart, black leather seating arranged around shiny black tables. And the old red carpet she remembered had become an expanse of wood laminate flooring. Duncan was standing at the bar with his back to her, talking to a couple she didn't recognise. The woman noticed her and tapped Duncan's arm. He swung round and smiled, coming forward to draw her into the company. He introduced the couple as Eileen and Brian Faulds.

The woman held out her hand for Kerra to shake.

'I'm the receptionist at the Health Centre,' she explained.

Kerra smiled and nodded.

'Are you joining us for dinner?'

It had been a perfectly reasonable assumption, but Eileen's cheeks coloured.

'Oh, no. Brian and I only called in for a drink.'

'Called in to be nosy, more like,' Brian said, glancing round the room. 'We haven't been in since the renovations. They've made a few changes. I hardly recognised the place.'

'Exactly what I was thinking,' Kerra said, wrinkling her nose. 'I kind of liked it the old way.'

The man smiled, ready to agree when a young waitress appeared at their side to tell them their table was ready whenever they were. Kerra and Duncan excused themselves, following the waitress to a table at the side of the room. The place was cold and she gave an involuntary shiver. The new owner of the Crofters' Arms had ruthlessly stripped out every semblance of traditional Highland hotel in favour of clinical, contemporary smartness.

The menus they were presented with were also tall, black, glossy affairs and Kerra raised an eyebrow at the prices. Then her gaze travelled around the room again and she realised that only one other table was occupied. She turned back to Duncan, who was still studying the menu.

He looked up and caught her watching him. For a split second their eyes locked, then she dropped her gaze, embarrassed. He switched his attention back to the menu.

'Does this meet with your approval?' he asked, smiling.

She hadn't thought the choice of dishes was anything special, but she returned his smile and nodded.

'Well, you're the expert,' he said. 'What would you recommend?'

His remark took her by surprise, although why it should have, she had no idea. He was bound to have asked Fiona about her. She wondered how much else she had told him.

They made their choices from the menu and Duncan ordered a bottle of wine. Their food arrived, and they ate in companionable silence. It was better than Kerra had expected. When the dessert trolley appeared, they declined, preferring to have cheese and biscuits with their coffee.

Duncan sat back, watching her. His gaze was disturbing and, to cover her discomfort, she said, 'Fiona never mentioned she had a brother.'

'She has two of us, actually. Colin is younger than me.'

He gave her a lazy smile. 'About your age.'

Kerra felt herself blush.

'I don't remember any of you from school.'

'That's probably because we were still living in Aberdeen then. Then the folks got the chance of this little smallholding just the other side of

Afferton and jumped at the opportunity. They weren't getting any younger and I suppose Dad saw it as a chance of easing up on the work.

'I wouldn't call running a smallholding easy work,' Kerra said, remembering how exhausted her father often was when he came in after a day's planting.'

Duncan grinned.

'I think they found that out, but they seem happy.'

'And do you live with them?' she asked.

He looked up at her so quickly that she realised how prying her question might have seemed. She had allowed herself to relax in his company, but they were still virtual strangers.

He let out a long sigh.

'I did for a few weeks after I came back. I've rented a place of my own now, nearer the Health Centre here in Craigallen.'

Kerra was trying to work out why he wanted to live near the Health Centre. He certainly didn't look ill.

'At the moment it's only locum work, of course, filling in for Doctor Grant while he's on extended leave, but I'm hoping for something more permanent soon.'

So that was it. He was a doctor! He obviously assumed she knew. But she did know Malcolm Grant. He had been her family's GP for as long as she could remember, and like everyone else in Craigallen she'd heard the rumours that he would be retiring when he returned from his world cruise with his wife. She realised Duncan was still talking.

'I've been in Africa,' he said. 'I worked for a children's charity. We were based in a hospital miles from nowhere, but walking long distances was nothing to the people there. They would come for miles to get their children treated.'

His eyes gazed out across the room and she knew that in his mind, he was back in Africa.

'You wouldn't believe how poor these families are. They exist on practically nothing.' He paused for a few seconds then said, 'Fiona tells me you're a chef.'

The change of topic wrong-footed her and she frowned.

'I'm sorry.' He jumped in quickly. 'We weren't talking about you, or anything.'

She met his eyes and they both burst out laughing. Duncan put up his hands.

'OK, so we were talking about you — but not gossiping.'

'It's all right. I believe you.' She giggled. 'And yes, I am a chef, which is why I'm setting up this new catering business.' She glanced across at him. 'I presume Fiona told you about that?'

'She did,' he said, his eyes on her. 'It's quite a courageous thing to do.'

She got the impression he'd been searching for the right word but settled for something more acceptable to her instead.

'Well, I suppose that's better than outright disapproval. My parents are a bit sceptical of me making a success of it.' She threw a glance around the

51

room. 'They think I'd be causing trouble for myself if I was to take any business away from this place.'

The couple across the room were getting up to leave. Duncan's eyes followed them out.

'They don't exactly seem to have cornered the catering market around here,' he said.

'Exactly,' Kerra said, and spent the next ten minutes enthusing about her plans. She was suddenly aware of how closely he had been watching her and another annoying blush began to creep over her face. 'I've been prattling on, haven't I?' she said. 'Sorry.'

He put up a hand.

'No, I love your enthusiasm. If it's any consolation, Fiona is as excited about the project as you are.'

'I was having a look round the prospective premises when we met earlier.'

'And what was the verdict?

She couldn't stop the wide grin that reached her eyes. Duncan smiled back, thinking she reminded him of a child who had just blown out the candles on her birthday cake.

She clasped her hands.

'It's perfect. We have to install a commercial kitchen in the back premises, and there's the little matter of turning the front shop into a tearoom. The current lease doesn't run out until the end of the month, but the couple who run the fashion shop are being co-operative.' She sighed. 'All I have to do now is sell my uncle's property in Inverness.'

'At the risk of chucking a bucket of water over your plans, I can't see that happening in the space of a month.'

'It doesn't matter, because Mr McAlpine, who owns the property, has agreed to let me have a six-month lease with an option to buy at the end of it.'

They hadn't noticed the approach of the tall, dark-haired man who'd come up to their table, and they looked up in surprise when he gave a polite cough. Kerra wondered how much of her comments he had heard.

'Was everything all right for you this evening?' He offered a professional smile.

Kerra nodded, taking in the dark grey suit, crisp purple-striped shirt and tie.

'The food was very nice,' she said.

Duncan nodded his agreement.

The man smiled, revealing a row of dazzling white teeth. He was looking at her in a way that made Kerra feel uncomfortable.

'Then perhaps you would be kind enough to pass the word around.' He waved his arm around the room. 'As you can see, it's all very new, but I'm sure people will soon get to hear about us.' He looked at Kerra. 'But I'm forgetting my manners.' He gave a peculiar little bow and offered his hand. 'Murray Glenn,' he said. 'I own this place.'

They took it in turns to shake the hand of the man who told the locals they were no longer welcome at the

Crofters' Arms. She wondered how long it would be before he was begging them to come back.

'I'm trying to place that accent. You're not from around here, Mr Glenn,' Duncan observed.

'You're right. I'm from Edinburgh originally, although that was in another life. I've been based in London for the past the few years . . . in hotel management.' He allowed himself another satisfied glance around the room.

The young waitress reappeared with their bill and, just for a second, Kerra thought the man was going to pick it up and tell them it was on the house. The thought had evidently crossed Duncan's mind, too, for he grabbed the slip of paper and handed the girl his credit card before Murray Glenn was aware what was happening. She suppressed a smile. Dr Crombie obviously had no intention of being in this man's debt. At least they shared that view. Bill paid, they got up to leave.

'Enjoy the rest of your evening,' Murray Glenn called after them. Kerra could feel his eyes still on her as they headed for the door.

Duncan was thoughtful when they emerged into the street.

'Penny for them,' Kerra said playfully as they walked towards her car.

'I was thinking about your business plan,' he said quietly. 'Being a great cook doesn't necessarily mean you can run a catering business.'

She glanced up at him quickly, unsure how to take the comment. But he wasn't finished.

'If my sister is going to invest in this thing then I think you should make her a partner.'

Kerra stopped dead and stared at him.

'Who says she's going to invest in my business?'

'She told me she offered to put up the five thousand pounds that's coming to her from your uncle's will. I would call that investment, wouldn't you?'

She faced him, her eyes blazing.

'You think I would take your sister's money? Fiona is a friend. She made that offer in a gesture of friendship. But just for the record, Doctor Crombie — ' Her voice was rising. 'If I accepted any money from her — which I have absolutely no intention of doing — it would be on a business footing.'

He put up his hands, and to Kerra's fury there seemed to be a glint of amusement in the grey eyes.

'Hold your horses, I wasn't suggesting you would rip her off. I'm just looking after my little sister's interests.'

'Well, as far as I'm concerned, she doesn't need your interference. Neither of us do!' She glared up at him before turning on her heel and marching off in the direction of her car, leaving him to stare after her.

An Offer Of Help

Duncan stood in the High Street, frowning down at the pavement, trying to work out why he'd behaved like that. His sister's mention that she'd offered Kerra her bequest money had taken him by surprise, then he felt his anger rising. Surely the woman would realise Fiona was just being kind. She could no more afford to hand over £5,000 for what, at best, could be a shaky financial venture. From what he'd heard, the young woman in question knew nothing about business. He'd every right to suggest caution.

In his heart he knew that the real reason he'd invited Kerra to dinner had been to warn her off, but after spending the evening together he'd decided that Kerra Morrison might not, after all, be the kind of young woman to take advantage of people.

It was the man who'd really annoyed him. He hadn't liked Murray Glenn's arrogance, or the way he had looked at Kerra. But then, she had done nothing to discourage him. If anything, he thought he'd caught a glint of amusement in her dark-blue eyes. He glanced back at the lighted windows of the Crofters' Arms, still seeing that look of invitation in Glenn's eyes, and shuddered.

He remembered how Kerra's face had lit up, and how her eyes sparkled as she outlined her plans. She wouldn't have discussed them in such detail if she hadn't trusted him — and now he'd behaved like an idiot. To make matters worse, she'd probably tell Fiona.

He'd only been back in the country a couple of months and here he was, already putting everyone's backs up. It seemed it was what he did best. He knew he was a good doctor, and that there had been no animosity towards him when he took over Dr Grant's patient list, but at the moment he was only a stand-in until their much-respected GP returned. If, as he hoped, he was invited to join the practice as a permanent member then he would have to win everyone's confidence on his own merit.

He'd been walking briskly, hardly noticing the extra effort of climbing the steep hill to his cottage, but when he reached the front door he glanced back over the roofs of the High Street properties. Had it been a mistake to come back to Craigallen? He couldn't change the past. But could he at long last live with it? He wasn't sure.

★ ★ ★

Kerra's head was still pounding with fury as she drove up the rutted track to the family farm. They'd been having such a great evening. But it was perfectly clear to her now that the only reason he had invited her to dinner was to check out her suitability to work with his sister. She'd obviously failed the test.

She was still harbouring a grievance about the previous night's unpleasant little scene outside the hotel when she walked into the kitchen next morning. Her mother, in a bright, floral apron, was standing at the ancient Aga, a pan of sizzling eggs and bacon in front of her.

'I'm about to call Dad in,' she said over her shoulder. 'Want me to stick a couple of rashers on for you?'

When there was no response, she looked round questioningly at her daughter.

'Everything all right, Kerra?'

Kerra looked up, frowning. She'd still been going over that exchange between her and Duncan Crombie.

'I'm fine, Mum.' She forced her brightest smile. 'Still half asleep, that's all,' she said, glancing at the glistening food that her mother was transferring to a warm plate. She went to the fridge and took out a carton of orange juice.

'I'll pass on that cooked breakfast.' She held up the carton. 'This'll be fine.'

'Ah.' Rosemary Morrison grinned. 'Too much rich food last night, is that it?'

Kerra avoided her mother's glance, wishing now that she hadn't mentioned last night's dinner invitation.

'I didn't realise you knew Doctor Crombie,' her father had said at the time. She hadn't missed the approving look that shot between her parents.

'He's Fiona's brother,' she had explained. 'It didn't seem right to refuse. Besides, he's taking me to the Crofters' Arms.' She'd thrown them a grin. 'I thought it would be a good opportunity to check out the opposition.'

Kerra concentrated now on pouring her juice, aware of her mother's worried expression as she watched her.

'The food wasn't bad,' she said, trying to keep her tone casual. 'Maybe a bit too fancy for Craigallen folk.'

'Were there many people there?'

Rosemary asked.

'Only one other couple, as far as I could see.' She paused. 'We did meet the owner, though. Murray Glenn. He came across to our table to introduce himself.' She gave an ironic smile and watched as her mother popped her father's breakfast in the oven. 'I don't believe the Crofters' Arms will be much competition for me.'

They both turned as the back door into the kitchen swung open with its familiar creak and Fraser Morrison came in. He brought with him the smell of the fields and the freshness of the morning.

'I could smell the bacon all the way across the yard.' He grinned, coming to give mother and daughter each a quick peck on the cheek.

He went to the sink to wash his hands before settling himself at the table, and then rubbed his newly scrubbed hands in anticipation of the appetising breakfast Rosemary was putting in front of him.

'How did it go with you and the young doctor last night?' he asked between mouthfuls of food.

'They met Murray Glenn,' Rosemary cut in before her daughter could speak. 'Kerra doesn't think he will be much competition for her catering business.'

Fraser looked up, cutlery poised.

'I wouldn't underestimate that one if I were you.' He caught his daughter's expression of protest, adding, 'Oh, I know you can look after yourself, Kerra. But this man doesn't play by the rules. That's what I've heard.'

Kerra remembered the appraising, if slightly insolent look Murray Glenn had given her last night. She'd no intention of underestimating the man. She got up and went round the table to squeeze her father's shoulders.

'He doesn't worry me, Dad.' It's Dr Duncan Crombie that I'm still trying to figure out, she thought. But she kept the thought to herself.

There was one more major task that still needed Kerra's attention before she could give all her concentration to the new venture — and she wasn't looking forward to it one bit.

Marcus le Bonn had trusted her enough to make her second in command in the kitchen of his busy Glasgow bistro. Now she had to tell him she was leaving. Would he see this as an insult? Accuse her of throwing his trust in her back in his face? She drew a deep breath. She hoped Marcus knew her better than that. But she did owe him a huge debt of thanks. He'd been like an adoptive father to her these past three years.

She tried to picture his reaction when she told him she was leaving. His arms would no doubt fly up in the familiar flamboyant gesture, and in the heavy French accent, that Kerra knew was not his own, he would utter some exaggerated phrase of distress. It was all part of the persona he'd adopted as the owner of a prestigious French restaurant. But Kerra knew the dark eyes, like shiny buttons, would not be able to hide their disappointment.

On her way to Glasgow she called in at Sinclair's shop to see Fiona and apprise her of the arrangements she had made with Jock McAlpine about his shop in Craigallen. The younger girl's face lit up and she danced a little jig behind the counter.

'Is it really going to happen?' she asked, eyes shining.

Kerra nodded, laughing.

'Not only that, but Mr McAlpine has agreed to let me lease the shop for six months before committing myself to buy.' Her eyes travelled over the bales of colourful fabrics on the shelves behind the counter of the premises. 'It'll probably take longer than that to sell this place, but at least it takes a bit of the pressure off.'

'Does that mean we could be up and running before the end of the summer?' Fiona asked.

'Oh, long before that, I hope. I'm off to Glasgow now to hand in my notice,' she said with a grin. 'We could have a tearoom up and running in about six weeks' time.'

Fiona clapped her hands and let out a little squeal as Kerra headed, laughing, for the door.

'I'll keep in touch,' she called back as she went out.

The one thing she hadn't mentioned was Fiona's brother's accusations of the previous night. She wasn't sure if she was more annoyed by the unfairness of his comments or the fact that he had spoiled an otherwise lovely evening.

Kerra made good time on her drive back to Glasgow and it was just after lunchtime when she arrived at her flat. The place smelled musty after having been closed up for so many days, and she went to open the windows, letting in the sound of the busy traffic below.

Desperate for a mug of coffee, she filled the kettle. Being back in the city was already making her feel edgy, or maybe that was because she wasn't looking forward to telling Marcus she was leaving. To say he would be devastated might be an exaggeration, but he would certainly make it appear that way. Marcus enjoyed the histrionics of a situation. He was a red-blooded Frenchman, after all, as he never tired of saying. She smiled, much as she adored Marcus le Bonn, he was no more French than her late, and much-loved, Granny Morrison, who had managed a Highland croft single-handed for at least ten years after Kerra's grandad died.

Marcus's real name was Simon Barnes — she'd seen it once on a tax return, which he'd snatched away. Being French gave him an air of intrigue, not to mention added kudos to his charisma as a great chef.

She sipped her coffee standing by the open window watching the congestion that had suddenly built up in the street below and suddenly longed to be back in Craigallen. She'd promised herself to put all thoughts of Duncan out of her mind, but here she was again remembering the intensity in those grey eyes as she told him about her business plans.

The muffled sound of her mobile in her bag made her start and she rummaged for it. Marcus's name flashed up on the tiny screen. She pulled a face and let it ring.

An hour later, after a shower, change of clothes and a fresh application of make-up, Kerra stared at her reflection in the mirror. She'd caught up her long, pale hair in a loose clip at the back of her head. But she still looked tired, and pinched her cheeks hoping to encourage a healthier glow. She knew what Marcus's first remarks would be when he saw her — and she was right.

'You look all in, little one,' he drawled, tilting his head to give her a chastising look.

Kerra dragged a stool from under the counter in the gleaming stainless steel restaurant kitchen, where staff were busy clearing up after a busy lunchtime trade. She perched uneasily on it.

'I need to tell you something, Marcus.'

He was covering a bowl of left-over tomato slices with a plastic film and looked up.

'Sounds serious, my pet.'

His eyes had dropped to where she was unconsciously twisting her fingers.

'The thing is, Marcus . . . I'm leaving.'

As predicted, Marcus's small dark eyes widened in an expression of disbelief.

'Leaving?' He shook his head. 'I don't understand. What do you mean?'

Kerra's shoulders rose in a helpless shrug. She'd known this wasn't going to be easy.

'Have you got another job?' he went on.

'Not in the way you mean.' She drew a deep breath. 'My uncle Sinclair has left me his business.'

Marcus stared at her, his brow knotted.

'I thought your uncle had a gents' outfitters?'

Kerra nodded.

'That's right. I mean he obviously didn't mean for me to run it. He left it for me to sell.' She grinned at him.

The chef let out a long sigh.

'You're giving up your career to live on an inheritance?'

He spoke the word as though it was an insult.

She shook her head, unable to keep the glint of excitement from her eyes.

'I'm going to start my own catering business. I've got first refusal on a shop in Craigallen High Street, and it's big enough to include a tearoom.' She slipped off her stool and went over to him. 'Oh, Marcus,' she said pleadingly, 'please be happy for me. It's what I've always wanted. I really want to do this.'

He grimaced, but held his arms out to her.

'Come here, little one,' he said, his French accent slipping. 'It's not what I had hoped for you, but if it will make you happy then who am I to stand in your way?'

71

'Thank you, Marcus,' she said quietly. 'I knew you would understand. I will, of course, work out my notice.' She looked up at him. 'As much as you need.'

'No,' he said quickly. 'You must go as soon as you're ready. We can manage here.'

She reached up and kissed his cheek.

'You know I love you, don't you?'

He shooed her back to her stool.

'When you say you will marry me, that's when I'll know,' he said with a wicked glint.

It had been easier than she'd imagined. She'd thought Marcus would fly into one of his famous rages when she told him. This calm acceptance of the situation was unsettling. She cocked her head in his direction.

'You're up to something, Marcus.'

He stared back in wide-eyed innocence.

'*Moi?*' he said with an expression of exaggerated shock. 'And just when I was about to offer my help.'

'You're going to help me?' She was off her stool again.

'That's right,' he said calmly. 'You didn't imagine I would allow my little prodigy to sail into the big bad sea of business without my guiding hand on the tiller?'

She stared at him, wide-eyed.

'Well,' he went on. 'I will need to see these premises, of course, and there will be the equipment.' He gave her a fond look. 'You might cook like an angel, but I doubt if you have a clue where to get the best deal on a Bain Marie.'

'Marcus, are you saying you want to come back with me?' An incredulous grin was spreading across her face. 'But what about the bistro? Won't you be needed here?'

'I'll be calling it a holiday, my pet. And as for being needed here, don't you think I've trained my chefs well enough to look after my restaurant in my absence? How soon can we start for Craigallen?'

A Set Up

Marcus nodded his approval as they drove along Craigallen's High Street, but Kerra saw him frown as he glanced at the café.

'Is that your competition?' he remarked.

She smiled.

'Not really. Carlos does have a couple of tables where people can sit and have a coffee, but mostly he just sells ice-cream and sweets. His fish and chips are very popular around here, though, but he only fries up in the evenings.'

She nodded ahead to the Crofters' Arms.

'That's the only place I have concerns about. The owner is trying to build up his outside catering business.' She slid Marcus a glance and winced. 'He doesn't know anything about my plans, but I have the feeling he won't be pleased.'

Marcus rubbed his hands together.

'Excellent,' he said. 'A little healthy competition does no-one any harm.' He glanced around with an approving smile. It was Saturday morning and the High Street was buzzing with shoppers. 'I like your little town,' he said.

'This is the place I wanted to show you, Marcus,' Kerra said, pulling up outside the Forsyths' fashion boutique.

'This is it?' His voice went up an octave, and his eyes widened in surprise as he took in the window display. He waved a hand at the place.

'Just wait till you see inside.' Kerra smiled. She'd rung ahead, asking the Forsyths if they would mind if she turned up with a friend to have another look over the premises.

'Think space, Marcus,' she urged as they went in.

After a polite nod of greeting to the Forsyths, Marcus's eyes travelled over the room as Kerra thanked them for allowing the intrusion.

'It's fine. Just go through to the back

and take all the time you need,' Rory Forsyth said obligingly.

Marcus preceded Kerra into the rear of the premises and put a finger to his cheek.

'Well, it's spacious. I'll grant you that.' He began moving round the room, pointing at walls, indicating corners, reeling off items of catering equipment that could be placed in the various spaces.

He nodded.

'I suppose we can do something with this, but you're surely not planning to install expensive equipment before you actually own the premises, are you?'

Kerra nodded.

'The child is mad,' he muttered.

Kerra spread her hands.

'What can go wrong?'

'A million things, my pet, which is exactly why I am here.' He turned on his heel. 'Now, let us find this hotel I'm in need of food.'

Standing with Kerra in the Crofters' Arms, Marcus glanced around the pristine smartness as they waited for the young woman behind the desk to book him in.

'Well, what do you think?' Kerra hissed in his ear. She'd told him the history of the place and the new owner's reluctance to encourage local business.

Marcus pursed his lips.

'I think it's fine — for the city.' He opened his arms in an expressive gesture. 'But in the middle of nowhere — '

'This isn't nowhere,' Kerra cut in, a flash of anger in her eyes, and then she saw him snigger. 'You're teasing me. What do you really think?'

Marcus nodded.

'I agree with you. It's hardly the traditional Highland hostelry. But it's what I am used to, so I shall be comfortable enough here for the time being.'

After a brief conversation, the receptionist replaced the phone and informed Marcus that his room was not ready for occupation. Kerra saw his eyebrow arch in surprise and read his mind. It was lunchtime, and the hotel didn't look busy, yet the room wasn't ready. He turned to take Kerra's arm and escorted her into the dining-room.

'Not up to my standards, or yours for that matter,' he said, ignoring Kerra's raised eyebrow as he finished his meal and dabbed the corners of his mouth with the red paper napkin, 'but beggars can't be choosers. Anyway, when were you proposing to order your equipment, bearing in mind it could take up to six weeks before it arrives?'

Kerra spread her hands.

'What do you suggest? The Forsyths' lease doesn't run out until the end of the month.'

'We have to draw up plans,' Marcus said. 'We'll have to go back there to measure up, but the Forsyths look like an accommodating pair. Once I get the whole thing down on paper we'll be able to think more clearly.'

'I'm so grateful to you, Marcus. I

can't believe you're doing all this for me.'

He waved away her gratitude.

'We need a base, somewhere we can spread out.' He glanced across at the waitress clearing a table. 'Too many ears around here,' he said.

'No problem. I know just the place,' Kerra said.

Her parents' cottage was only a ten-minute drive away, and she'd rung ahead to tell them they were on their way. But there was still an embarrassed blush to Rosemary's cheeks as she extended her hand to Marcus, for instead of shaking it, he raised it to his lips and kissed it. Kerra rolled her eyes, but her mother's flush only deepened.

'And this is my father, Fraser Morrison,' she cut in quickly. The men shook hands with a nod to each other.

'You did say we could use the dining-room, Mum? It will only be temporary, but we need a base to work from.'

'Of course. Would you like tea,

Monsieur le Bonn?'

Kerra saw her father's hand go up to hide his grin.

'It's Marcus, dear lady. Let's not stand on ceremony.'

'Marcus,' Rosemary repeated, straightening her apron.

'Can we have it through in the dining-room, Mum? We want to get started.'

'You two go ahead.' Her mother smiled back. 'The tea won't take a minute to brew.'

Marcus glanced around the small dining-room.

'It's compact,' he commented.

'We only need the table,' Kerra said.

She lifted her laptop and reached for a couple of the large notebooks she had bought. Over the next two hours she and Marcus poured over their notes, jotting down ideas, essential equipment, details of how her catering operation should be run. They created spreadsheets, scheduled in costs and discussed how to market the new service.

The sound of pots being rattled in the kitchen told Kerra that her mother had already begun their evening meal.

'You will stay for tea, won't you?' she asked.

But he was already getting up, collecting the notebooks to take with him.

'Alas, no. I will get back to the hotel. I have much homework to do tonight. And, I haven't yet seen my room,' he reminded her.

Kerra's mother looked disappointed when she realised their guest would not be sharing their evening meal.

'It smells delicious,' Marcus said, sniffing the air with a look of bliss on his face. 'But perhaps I could come back another evening?'

It could have been her imagination, but Kerra thought her father looked relieved, so she nudged him as she passed, seeing Marcus out.

When she came back her eyes were shining.

'Well, what did you think of him? Isn't he great?'

'Yeah, great,' her father said bleakly.

Her mother was nodding enthusiastically.

'I liked him,' she said.

Kerra's head was still buzzing with plans and ideas as she helped her mother wash up. She needed to share her mood with someone just as enthusiastic as she was about the new business.

She went to find her phone.

'Fiona! I'm back. Fancy meeting up for a drink?'

The voice at the other end hesitated.

'That's a great idea. Do you know the Hare and Hound, just outside Craigallen, on the Inverness road?'

Kerra did, although she'd never been inside the place.

'Can you get there for around eight?' Fiona asked.

'No problem, I've got loads to tell you.'

Kerra was first to arrive and ordered

a glass of wine while she sat in a corner waiting for Fiona. But the person who walked in was not the one she was expecting.

'Duncan? What are you doing here?' Was it her imagination, or had his face just coloured?

He came across, looking as surprised as she was.

'I was supposed to be meeting my sister,' he said curtly, 'but she's just rung me to say she can't manage.'

Kerra's eyebrow arched.

'Same here,' she said. 'Fiona and I arranged to meet to discuss — ' she gave a little cough ' — the business.'

Duncan shook his head.

'What's the little minx playing at?' But he thought he already knew. He hadn't given his sister the details of their falling out. He knew she wouldn't have appreciated him standing up for her when there had been no need to. Kerra wasn't taking advantage of anyone. He knew that now. It didn't stop him feeling foolish, though.

He had called in at the shop when he'd been in Inverness the day after his dinner with Kerra. He had hoped to find her there. She was due an apology. The news that she'd gone to Glasgow and might not be back for a month sent his spirits plummeting. Now here she was, only a few feet away, not looking particularly pleased to see him.

'Now that we are both here, let me buy you another drink,' he offered.

But Kerra put her hand over the top of her glass.

'I have the car,' she said. 'One glass is enough.'

'Then would you mind if I bought myself a pint and joined you?'

For a moment he thought she was going to tell him to go away, then he saw the edges of her mouth twitch.

Her shoulders raised in a shrug.

'Why not,' she said.

Kerra watched him at the bar. It had been less than a week since she last saw him. He wasn't looking quite so confident tonight. He turned and caught her watching him and his face creased into a smile. Her heart gave an alarming thud.

He returned and put his pint on the table, sliding in beside her. He gave an uneasy little cough.

'I owe you an apology,' he said quietly, not looking at her. 'My behaviour the other night was disgraceful and I have no excuse for what I said.' He glanced up and caught her eye. 'I know you would never take advantage of Fiona, or anyone else for that matter.' He put his hands up. 'I don't know why I said it.'

The slow smile she remembered began to curve his mouth.

'Am I forgiven?'

She began to reach out for her glass, but her hand was trembling and she quickly put it back in her lap, hoping he hadn't noticed. She could forgive him just about anything when he looked at her like that.

'You're forgiven,' she said quietly. 'I take it your sister arranged this little meeting? Does that mean you discussed the other night with her?'

He took a deep drink of his beer and wiped away the foam moustache it left.

'She did arrange this, yes. But we never discussed what you're referring to. I would have been too ashamed. I don't think Fiona would have appreciated knowing about it.'

They fell silent and Kerra looked round the crowded bar.

'Mr Glenn should have left the Crofters' the way it was. He's missing out on all this.' She saw Duncan's jaw tighten and wondered what she'd said to annoy him.

'Fiona wasn't expecting you back from Glasgow for weeks yet,' he said.

'That's what I thought, too, but things didn't quite turn out that way.' She found herself telling Duncan about Marcus, and how he had waved aside her notice, then helped her escape from the legal confines of the lease on her flat by finding a new tenant to replace her. 'He's even come to Craigallen with me to help get things set up.'

'He must think a lot of you,' he said stiffly.

'It's mutual,' Kerra said, sliding him a curious glance.

'I suppose he's staying with you up at the farm?'

She shook her head.

'He's booked into the Crofters' Arms.'

She hadn't noticed they'd long since finished their drinks and the place was beginning to empty.

'I must get back,' she said, gathering up her things. 'There's lots to do tomorrow.'

'My surgery begins at eight,' Duncan said with a sigh, getting up and standing aside for her to brush past him.

It was easy to forget this good-looking man with the compelling grey eyes was a family doctor, with a surgery full of patients to deal with in the morning.

They walked together to the car park.

'I'll say goodnight, then,' she said, keeping her eyes down as she headed towards her car.

'Goodnight, Kerra,' he called after her.

* * *

Marcus was still at breakfast next morning when Kerra turned up at the hotel.

'Sleep well?' she asked, sitting opposite him, smiling as he clicked his fingers to call a waitress to fetch another cup and saucer for his guest.

'Tolerably so,' he said. But she could tell from his expression that he had settled into the Crofters' Arms.

He leaned forward conspiratorially, his eyes moving round the room to ensure he would not be overheard.

'I met Mr Glenn last evening,' His dark eyebrows drew together. 'Tricky man. Not to be trusted.'

Kerra sipped her tea. It wasn't the Earl Grey they had ordered, but this morning she wasn't bothered. They were on their way to Inverness to meet Fiona, and that young lady had a few things to explain. But the real purpose of the visit was for her to meet Marcus, and for him to give her a run down of what they had been planning.

They called in briefly at the Craigallen shop to ask the Forsyths if they would mind them returning later to take some measurements. They didn't and Kerra thanked them. She must remember to buy them a gift before they left.

Fiona was looking embarrassed when they walked in.

'I'm so sorry about last night, Kerra.'

Kerra raised an eyebrow and tried to keep a straight face. Duncan had obviously not spoken to her.

'Did you stay long waiting for me?' she asked, doing her best to sound innocent.

'It was after ten before we left, actually.'

'We?'

89

'Your brother and I. Don't look so innocent,' Kerra said. 'You set us up last night.'

Fiona's cheeks flooded with colour.

'I'm sorry, but I thought you two had things to discuss. Duncan called in here last week hoping to find you. I gather you two had words when you went to the Crofters' Arms. He looked so disappointed when I told him you might be away in Glasgow for weeks.'

So he had tried to find her. She had underestimated him. She was beginning to get the distinct feeling that maybe he wasn't so bad after all.

She introduced Marcus, who made Fiona giggle by giving a gracious little bow.

'Marcus is going to help us set things up.'

'Really?' Fiona's eyed widened. 'That's wonderful.'

Not many customers interrupted them as they outlined the plans they had made. The front shop would be stripped of its counter. Apart from decoration, there wouldn't be too much work to do, as the place was pretty much open plan already. They would check up on furniture prices and delivery dates. Most of the work would happen behind the scenes. The huge back room would have to be completely emptied to make way for the new appliances Marcus would order for the business.

Fiona put a hand to her head.

'I can't believe things are happening so fast.'

'We'll have to make arrangements to close the shop here, but if you wouldn't mind coming in as usual for the next few days then we can sort things out later.'

'Have you seen this?' Fiona asked, reaching for the weekly newspaper. 'The shop and tailoring business is advertised for sale here.'

Kerra nodded.

'It should be in the property pages of the nationals tomorrow. Let's hope we get some interest.'

A Helping Hand

They held a going-away party for the Forsyths. It was, at first, an awkward little gathering because although the couple were popular, they hadn't chosen the kind of business that Craigallen folk really needed. But once everybody relaxed, the evening started to go with a swing.

The evening went well. Marcus charmed all the ladies, and Jock McAlpine made a little speech of farewell to the Forsyths, adding a note of welcome and good wishes to Kerra and her new business. There were lots of handshakes and kissed cheeks, but eventually the room began to empty as people made to leave. Marcus made his way back to the Crofter's Arms, where no doubt Murray Glenn would be lying in wait to question him about the evening's events.

Fiona, Duncan and her parents were last to leave, and Kerra went outside to wave them off.

'Goodnight, Duncan,' she said crisply as he passed.

He stopped and turned to her, his eyes serious.

'Goodnight, Kerra.'

She swallowed a lump in her throat as she watched the small red car drive away out of the town.

'We're waiting for news of a little place we're hoping to lease in Inverness,' Daisy confided when Kerra went back to help the couple clear up after the party.

'But that's wonderful,' she enthused.

Daisy nodded.

'We stand a much better chance of success in the city. I know there are plenty of trendy young people in Inverness.' She saw Kerra's smile and rushed to explain. 'Not that the folks here are dowdy or anything.'

'I know what you mean, Daisy.' She laughed. 'I agree. The flair for fashion that you and Rory have is wasted in a place like this. You'll do brilliantly well in Inverness.'

'Keep your fingers crossed for us,' Daisy said, turning to rinse the glasses in the sink.

Daisy and Rory had hired a big van and taken all their stock away the day before. Only a few of their personal things remained to be collected.

'Will you be sorry to leave?' Kerra asked.

Daisy shook her head.

'Craigallen is a nice little town, but it wasn't for us. This is your place now, Kerra.' She came to squeeze her hand. 'And I know you will make a go of it.'

She remembered the words as she stood on the pavement that night waving the Forsyths off. What did it matter if Duncan Crombie chose to be aloof? She had bigger fish to fry. This really was her place now! She hugged herself. She really would make a go of it!

94

Marcus was waiting in reception at the Crofters' Arms when Kerra came to drive him to the railway station in Inverness. The door behind the desk into the office was ajar and she could see Murray inside.

'So you're leaving us again,' he said, coming forward to shake Marcus's hand.

'A temporary situation. I shall be back on Wednesday.'

'Well, I'm glad to hear it.' He turned his attention to Kerra. 'I understand congratulations are in order. I meant to call in at your little gathering to wish you luck last night.' He extended his arms and glanced around him. 'But you know what it's like when you're in business.'

She didn't remember inviting him to the 'little gathering', but she inclined her head anyway.

'A tearoom, I understand,' he persisted. 'How soon will you have it up and running?'

The man was fishing for information and Kerra had no intention of accommodating him. She shrugged and gave him a helpless smile.

'This is all new to me, Mr Glenn. I might well be coming to you for advice.'

She saw Marcus conceal a grimace.

'Feel free to seek me out any time at all — and the name's Murray, by the way.'

Kerra could feel his eyes on her back as they walked out of the door and into the High Street.

'You've got him worried,' Marcus said as they climbed into the car. 'I think you will have to watch that one.'

Kerra's mood was so euphoric that she ignored the remark. Yes, there was still plenty to do, but the bank had given the go ahead for a bridging loan until the Inverness shop was sold. The painters would move in on Monday morning, and if all went well, they'd be finished by Thursday.

In Inverness she pulled into the station car park and together they walked to the platform.

'I have something for you,' Marcus said, lifting his case onto a bench and sliding out a familiar catering magazine, which he handed to Kerra. 'Page forty-eight.'

With a sigh, she flicked through the pages, stopping at the relevant one.

'It's a hotel sale.' She frowned, running her eye down the list of items to go under the hammer. Then her face broke into a smile.

'It's all here,' she said. 'Everything we need is for sale right here.'

'Yes, my angel. Your fairy godfather looks after you.'

Kerra threw her arms around him just as the Glasgow train arrived at the platform.

'Thank you, Marcus. I don't know what I would have done over the past weeks without you.'

'Just get some good stuff at that sale,' he said, climbing on the train and turning for a final wave. 'Keep in touch.'

Fiona was already waiting outside the shop when Kerra got back to Craigallen. It was mid-morning and the Saturday shoppers were out in force. She parked in the rear yard and hurried through to open the street door for Fiona.

'I'm not happy about closing the draper's today, Kerra. This is our busiest day,' Fiona said as she swept past her into the empty front shop.

'I need you here,' Kerra said, her eyes shining. 'I have news.'

She pulled out the catering magazine and thumbed through the pages until she found what she was looking for.

'It's an omen,' she said, pointing to the half-page advertisement. 'Everything we need is up for grabs here.' She let out a long breath. 'And to think I was planning to buy everything new. We can save a fortune.'

Fiona caught Kerra's mood.

'This is brilliant. It says there are

98

tables and chairs, and there's a coffee machine, and crockery and cutlery.' Her face was radiant. 'This is wonderful. I take it you know how to go about all this auction stuff?'

Kerra shook her head, laughing.

'Never been to one, but that's not going to stop me.'

'Right,' Fiona said, dragging a couple of stools from behind the counter. 'What do we have to do first?'

Plans were whizzing around Kerra's head and she tried to collect them into some kind of order.

'The Castlecrag Hotel is in Pitlochry and the sale is on Wednesday, so I need you to stay here for the painters.'

Fiona nodded.

'I expect the successful bidders will be expected to take the items away with them on the day, which means we will need a van,' Kerra said thoughtfully.

'Can you drive a van?' Fiona asked.

'No need,' a voice said. 'I'm coming with you.'

Both women turned. They hadn't

locked the shop door and hadn't heard Duncan come in.

'If you want the extra help, that is,' he said.

'Of course we do, Duncan.' Fiona turned to Kerra, 'Don't we?'

Kerra tried to blink back her surprise.

'I . . . I'm not sure,' she said hesitantly.

'So you can heave a dozen tables and fifty chairs into the back of a van on your own, not to mention all the heavy kitchen stuff?' He came across the shop to join them, 'Sorry if I'm jumping the gun, it's just that I heard you talking. But if you don't want my help . . . ' He shrugged.

'What about your surgery?' Kerra cut in.

He gave her a laconic grin.

'Even doctors get a day off.'

As it happened, Duncan did more than offer to drive, he organised the lease of their vehicle. The sale wasn't due to start until ten o'clock, but they'd planned to arrive at Pitlochry by eight-thirty to give Kerra time to view the stock and select the things she wanted to bid for. Duncan said it would be a two-hour drive, so they arranged to meet in Craigallen's High Street at six a.m.

Her first glimpse of the van made Kerra gasp.

'It's huge,' she said. 'Do we need a vehicle this big?'

'I don't know,' Duncan said. 'Doesn't that rather depend on what you buy?'

It was a reasonable comment and she climbed, unassisted, into the passenger seat. Sitting next to him as the van sped along the country roads was like being on top of the world. At this height Kerra could see over hedges to the colourful expanse of fields that criss-crossed the landscape. A white mist was clinging to the valleys, but Kerra knew it would soon burn off once the sun got to work on it.

The roads were still quiet as they drove into Pitlochry. The Castlecrag

Hotel perched majestically at the top of a wooded hill overlooking the town. Duncan drove into the car park, and Kerra frowned at the collection of other assorted vans. She was obviously to have some stiff competition in today's auction.

They got out and climbed the few stairs into the hotel. A large hand-painted board directed them to the vast dining-room where the auction would be held. Kerra looked around the room in dismay. It seemed like every available corner had been packed with stuff. She'd no idea where to begin. She wished Marcus was here.

'Look,' Duncan said, touching her arm. 'I'll see if I can find us a couple of coffees while you have a nose around.'

'I don't know where to start,' she said helplessly. Whatever had made her think she could do this?

Duncan was watching her, his brows knitted. Then he scanned the room.

'The thing is not to let it overwhelm you. Look.' He pointed to where the stainless-steel kitchen items were displayed. 'There's a pattern. Each category has its own section.' He nodded towards rows of armchairs, bedroom furniture, tables stacked with crockery.

She nodded and looked up at him. His steady grey eyes were still concerned. Her hand closed over his.

'I'll be fine. I can do this,' she said, smiling.

For a second he didn't move, and Kerra realised she was still touching his hand. She flushed and looked away, rummaging in her bag for the notebook she'd brought.

'I'll get that coffee,' he said, turning and striding away.

It was nerves that were making her feel so vulnerable. She would have to pull herself together. She was here to do a job, and the whole future of her new business could depend on how successful she was today.

In Duncan's absence she began to wander, getting her bearings. She'd made a list of all the items she needed and began to work her way around the various sections, jotting down catalogue numbers as she went. Then she stopped. Catalogue! She needed a catalogue! She turned to the door and almost collided with Duncan, who had returned, a plastic cup of coffee in each hand.

'Is this what you're looking for?' He grinned, nodding down to the shiny green catalogue tucked under his arm. He saw the look on her face and his grin widened.

'I know,' he said. 'Do you think anyone's noticed that we're amateurs at this auction lark?'

She slid the catalogue from under his arm, and took one of the coffees.

'You think of everything,' she said happily.

She scanned the pages, marking the items of interest, then set about tracking them down in the room. There was less than an hour's viewing time left.

'Can I do anything to help?' Duncan asked.

'You can be my consultant if you like.' She grinned back at him and raised an eyebrow at his expression. 'No, seriously. I need a second pair of eyes to convince me I won't be bidding for rubbish. Take this, for instance.' She stopped before a collection of small square tables that seemed ideal for the tearoom. 'I wouldn't recognise wood-worm if it came up and introduced itself.'

'And you think I would?'

'I think you recognise quality when you see it, Duncan.' It was the first time she had used his name and they were both aware of it.

'I'll take that as a compliment,' he said.

By the time Kerra had ticked off most of the items in her 'wanted' list, the buyers were taking their places. When the auctioneer moved in behind his podium, her heart was racing. She took a quick glance around the room.

'These people all look as if they know what they're doing,' she murmured.

To her amazement she felt Duncan's arm go around her and give her shoulders a squeeze.

'You can do this.' He smiled encouragingly.

She looked up at him.

'Actually, Duncan, will you do the bidding for me?' She wondered why she hadn't thought of it before.

'Are you sure?'

She nodded.

'Definitely.' She passed across the catalogue where she had jotted down the items she wanted to bid for, and the limits she was prepared to pay. His jaw tightened and she saw him swallow. Poor Duncan. He was probably as nervous as she was. Maybe it wasn't fair to force this responsibility on him. She glanced up at him.

He gave a nervous laugh.

'Well, if you trust me, I could always have a go.'

The first lot was crockery — cups,

saucers, and plates — all perfect for the tearoom. The bidding didn't even come close to Kerra's limit. The hammer came down and the auctioneer pointed to Duncan.

'You did it!' Kerra whispered, tugging at his sleeve.

They had similar success with the tables and chairs they had selected. Not all of the big catering items came their way, but by the end of the day Kerra was satisfied with her purchases. Duncan was looking pleased with himself, too.

'I think you really enjoyed that,' she said, nudging him with a mischievous grin.

'You do realise we've bought an awful lot of stuff?'

He watched as she hugged herself.

'I know. Isn't it great?'

'Yeah, great,' he repeated, grimacing. 'If you totter off and join that queue of people waiting to pay for their purchases, I'll go and find how we collect your stuff.'

The next couple of hours seemed like organised chaos to Kerra, as everyone located the items they had bought and carried them out to an assembled fleet of vans. One person had even turned up driving a tractor and was loading bedroom furniture onto a trailer.

'This will take for ever.' She sighed as she and Duncan struggled to lift a heavy stainless-steel oven into the back of their hired van. She watched him push back the shiny brown hair that had flopped over his forehead. His face was glistening with sweat and she felt a rush of guilt.

'I have an idea,' he said suddenly, stretching his back and rubbing his grubby palms down his jeans. He jumped down from the van. 'You stay here,' he told her, striding across the car park.

Ten minutes later, he was back, accompanied by a porter, who was stuffing the £20 note Duncan had slipped him into his pocket. He'd brought a mini forklift truck.

'How did you manage that?' she asked, gaping.

'Where there's a will . . . ' He smiled sweetly at her.

She shook her head. Duncan Crombie was quite unlike any man she had ever known. The porter lost no time in climbing into the van and rearranging the heavy equipment. Kerra was so busy marvelling at the man's efficiency, she wasn't aware of Duncan's eyes on her.

'You're very quiet,' Kerra said as they later shared a pub meal of steak and kidney pie. She'd noticed the change in him as soon as they'd left Pitlochry and wondered what was wrong. She glanced round the dining area. They couldn't have chosen better. Candles had been placed on each table and the low murmur of conversation, combined with the wine, was putting her in a very relaxed mood.

She glanced at him across the flickering flame and her heart gave a lurch. He caught her looking at him and sat back, pushing his plate aside.

'Sorry, I've been bad company. Tomorrow is the monthly practice conference. I've been going over in my head some of the issues that are likely to crop up.' Even to him it sounded like a lame excuse, but what could he say? He could hardly tell her he was in danger of becoming seriously involved — not when he was determined to nip these feelings in the bud. He forced a smile. 'You did well today, I was proud of you. Have you saved lots of cash?'

Kerra nodded, her face animated again.

'A huge amount,' she said. 'And now things can go ahead faster then I'd thought. If I'd bought everything new then it could have taken six weeks to arrive.' Her eyes went to the window, and the van that was packed with her new equipment. 'There's enough in there to get the tearoom up and running. As soon as the decorators are finished, we will be ready for business.' Her face was glowing.

The sun was sinking in the evening sky, casting a mellow gold across the hills as they drove home. In different circumstances it could have been romantic, but they'd fallen into another uneasy silence. She slid him a quick glance. His handsome profile was composed as he concentrated on the road, but there was a tension to his jaw, and once Kerra thought she'd seen his muscles tighten.

She bit her lip and looked away. He'd done his good deed for the day and now he obviously wanted to get back — and as far away from her as possible.

She should have learned after that first dinner. From now on she would keep her distance from Duncan Crombie.

'Something's Wrong'

'I can't believe all this is really happening.' Fiona stood in the middle of what would soon be the Craigallen Tearoom and hugged herself.

Kerra paced the room, looking around her.

'They've made a good job of the decorating. All we have to do now is move the tables and chairs through here and we're sorted.'

In addition to the several boxes of crockery and cutlery she'd bought at the hotel sale, Kerra had managed to acquire a collection of cake stands, tea and coffee-making machines. She'd sketched out some advertisements that would go in the local newspaper, and some of the local shops had agreed to put up posters for the tearoom's grand opening.

That afternoon she was interviewing

potential staff for both the tearoom and the outside catering side of things. She hoped she would be able to conceal just how nervous she was feeling about that.

Fiona nodded towards the back premises where, judging by the banging and sawing they could hear, the workforce Kerra had employed to fit out her shiny, nearly new commercial kitchen were not wasting time.

'When will that lot be finished?' She'd popped her head round the door when she arrived at eight that morning and the contractors were already hard at work.

'They've promised it will all be completed by tomorrow,' Kerra said, unable to stop the wide grin. 'It's all happening so quickly I can hardly believe it. But if the work in the kitchen is as good as the decorators have done in here then I won't be complaining.'

'I know. Isn't it great?' Fiona said, her eyes taking in the fresh cream walls, the newly painted counter, with its sparkling glass cases where the cakes and scones would be displayed. Tea and coffee-making equipment was on a specially made counter on the back wall. Jock McAlpine had only recently had the oak laminate floor laid, and it now looked just about perfect.

'We could bring those tables and chairs in now, Kerra,' Fiona suggested, unable to conceal her excitement.

The tearoom wouldn't be officially opening for another week, but it would be another job out of the way.

'Let's do it,' Kerra agreed.

An hour later, both women slumped into chairs, looking around at the results of their efforts. They had a proper tearoom at last. It only needed the addition of the pretty red gingham tablecloths Fiona's mother had made and bowls of fresh garden flowers, and the place would be as welcoming as any tearoom Kerra had ever known.

The next week passed in a blur of activity. A young man by the name of Will Barnes, from Inverbeg, had been engaged as a catering assistant. He'd worked in a hotel in Inverness and had been looking for a new challenge. Kerra's Catering, as she'd now named the business, would certainly offer him that. Two local women, Janie Campbell and Tina Stone, had been taken on as waitresses, but both agreed to help out in the kitchen when necessary.

Kerra had determinedly put any thoughts of Duncan out of her mind, so she'd been surprised when he walked into the tearoom just as she and Fiona were stacking the newly washed cups and saucers on the back shelves.

'That's what I like to see,' he said. 'Women working.'

Fiona swung round, picked up a tea towel and chucked it at her brother.

'I take it you haven't come to help,' she said.

'I thought the kettle might be on.' He smiled at Kerra.

Her heart gave an alarming lurch.

'It's the least you deserve after taking me to that auction,' she said, trying to keep the tremor out of her voice as she reached for the kettle. 'We hope to be a bit more professional for our grand opening on Monday.' She looked up quickly. 'You are coming?'

'Try keeping me away.' He grinned back.

Duncan was full of praise as he glanced around the room. And rightly so, Kerra thought. They had done well. She was quiet as the brother and sister chatted. Duncan asked about their parents.

'Mum and Dad are coming to the opening,' Fiona said.

Talk of their parents brought a sudden picture of Duncan in short trousers, a grazed knee from where he'd tumbled from a tree. Kerra could picture his hair falling over his face in the adorable way that it did when he was engrossed in something. She looked up to find his eyes thoughtfully on her face. For one uncomfortable moment she imagined he'd been able to read her thoughts. She felt her cheeks colour as she looked away.

'What about Marcus? Is he coming to our opening?'

Kerra realised with a start that Fiona was talking to her.

'Yes, of course. He's driving up this weekend.' She was feeling uncomfortable under Duncan's watchful gaze. Then, to her surprise, he reached across the table and took the mug from her hands, examining her face. 'You look tired, Kerra,' he said, and his expression was concerned.

She'd been so busy over the last few days she'd hardly stopped for a coffee, let alone a meal, and most of the food her mother cooked had stayed uneaten on her plate.

'You need feeding up. That's the problem,' he announced, standing up and reaching for Kerra's hand. 'You two are coming for lunch.'

Fiona looked at Kerra's startled face, then at her brother.

'I have quite a bit more to do in here this morning,' she said quickly. 'But you're right about Kerra. She definitely needs a break, and I can manage here on my own.'

'Well, it doesn't look like I have any choice,' Kerra said weakly. She was very aware that Duncan was still holding her hand and leading her towards the door.

Fiona grabbed Kerra's bag and thrust it into her hand.

'Have fun, you two,' she called after them as they crossed the road and got into the little red sports car.

They found a country pub, and judging by the number of vehicles in the car park, the place was popular. They made their way to the bar. Kerra was acutely aware of how awful she must look. She wasn't wearing a scrap of make-up and her hair must now be all over the place.

She escaped to the Ladies' for some quick repairs. After a quick wash, brush up, and application of pink lipstick, she felt more like her old self. It was with more confidence that she walked back into the bar to join Duncan.

As he led her to their table his

admiring glance confirmed that her efforts had not been wasted.

'Welcome back,' he said, grinning. 'I thought we had lost you for a while back then.'

She gave him a questioning look and he said, 'When I saw you in the tearoom, you looked worse than some of my patients.' He shot her a mischievous grin.

She gave an embarrassed smile and ran her eye down the list of dishes. Some of them were her own specialties, the ones that won her high praise at Marcus's Glasgow bistro. If she ordered one of these she would only be making comparisons.

'I'll have haggis,' she said, closing the menu.

'Good choice. I'll have the same.'

He went to the bar to order their food and she leaned back against the bench seat. No matter how hard she tried she would never understand this man. One minute she was certain he was interested in her, and in the next he'd turned cold. It was like he could switch affection on and off at will.

She caught sight of herself in a mirror on one of the posts that separated the different sections of the bar, and realised she was scowling. She made a concentrated effort to smile, unaware that Duncan had returned.

'That's better,' he said.

Suddenly Kerra threw her head back and laughed, and it was as though all the tension had drained from her.

'I've been a right pain, haven't I?' she said.

He nodded, grinning.

'But you're smiling again — and that was the point of the exercise.'

'Thank you, Duncan,' she said, meeting his eyes.

'All part of the service,' he said as their food arrived.

* * *

It was early afternoon when Marcus drove his silver Lexus out of Glasgow.

The Sunday traffic at the end of August was busy, but at least there were fewer lorries on the road.

By the time he reached Inverness the rain had settled to a damp drizzle, but in the distance he could see a sliver of blue sky. Half an hour later, he was pulling to a stop in front of the tearoom. The windows were festooned with red and gold posters, proclaiming the next day's grand opening. He'd noticed similar advertising in some of the other shops he'd passed. He smiled to himself. Kerra had been busy.

She rushed out to meet him before he was even through the door, linking arms and walking in with him.

'What do you think, Marcus?'

His eyes moved slowly around the room, taking in the cheerful red checked table linen, the fresh flowers, and the rows of gleaming cups, saucers and plates behind the counter and clasped his hands.

'I think it's wonderful, little one.'

Kerra beckoned Fiona to come over

and put an arm around her shoulders.

'I couldn't have managed all this without Fiona.'

The younger girl flushed, but she appreciated the praise.

'I think most of Craigallen is coming tomorrow. I just hope we have enough food.'

'The fridges are bulging.' Kerra laughed. 'Come through and see my new kitchen, Marcus.'

She led the way into the back premises, which had been little more than an empty shell the last time Marcus saw it. He spun round, clamping his hands to his face.

'You bought all this at auction?' His voice rose in amazement. 'You're amazing, you know that?' Glancing back to the door where Fiona stood, he added, 'Both of you, and I insist that you both join me for dinner.'

Marcus wasn't a man to be refused, so Kerra and Fiona found themselves in the back of his Lexus as he drove them to the Crofters' Arms car park.

The dining-room was busy, but Kerra didn't recognise any of the diners. They were shown to a table and when the menus arrived, Marcus recommended the beef stroganov, which they all ordered, with a bottle of robust red wine.

Kerra had chosen her moment to tell Marcus the best news of all.

'Matthew West rang me yesterday,' she started.

Marcus's eyebrow went up.

'Uncle Sinclair's solicitor,' she said.

'Ah, yes.' He nodded.

'Now, nothing has been signed yet, but I think we've sold the shop.'

* * *

It was dark by the time they had finished their meals and Marcus walked Kerra and Fiona back to the tearoom to collect their cars. Before they had even reached the place, Kerra stopped dead.

'Something's wrong,' she said, her voice shaking. She began to run and the others followed. Then they froze,

123

staring at the tearoom windows. The pristine orderliness they had left an hour earlier was now a scene of total chaos. Tables and chairs had been upturned, the walls daubed with graffiti, and the glass cake cabinets shattered.

Marcus put an arm around Kerra's shoulders.

'I'm sure it looks worse than it is. Let's have a look inside before we start to panic.'

Kerra stared through the glass at the chaos and put her hands to her head.

'How can it look worse than it is? It's wrecked,' she shrieked. Tears of sheer anger were pricking her eyes, but she was determined not to cry. 'Who could have done this, Marcus? Who hates me enough to do something like this?'

Fiona's hands were covering her face and Kerra could see the girl's shoulders shaking.

'Let's go inside,' Marcus urged. Kerra's hands trembled as she put the key in the lock.

Marcus went ahead to make sure the culprits were not still on the premises.

'They must have come in the back door.'

Kerra's hand flew to her mouth.

'My kitchen,' she said, and rushed past them into the kitchen. She reached for the light switch, hardly daring to open her eyes when the lights flickered on. She could hardly believe it. The place hadn't been touched.

Marcus had come up behind her and was staring into the kitchen. The tall, stainless-steel catering fridge, double ovens and gleaming sinks had not been damaged.

'Thank goodness,' he whispered under his breath.

They went back to the tearoom. Fiona was on her mobile.

'I've just called Duncan. He's coming over.'

Kerra nodded.

'Maybe we should call the police,' Fiona said.

But Kerra put up her hand. She was

feeling steadier now that the initial shock was wearing off.

'Let's wait for Duncan,' she said.

The three of them stood around, not sure what to do Then the shop door burst open and Duncan was there. He stared at the sight, an expression of disbelief on his face. At the sight of him, Fiona's resolve to stay strong crumpled and she ran sobbing to him. He held her, his eyes on Kerra.

He looked at Marcus.

'How did they get in?'

'The back door was forced,' Marcus said.

Kerra was standing in the middle of the chaos, a lost look in her eyes.

'I wasn't sure if I should call the police,' she said. Her voice sounded thin and shaky.

Duncan found an unbroken chair and sat Kerra down.

'Let's have a look round first to see if we can salvage any of this.' He began to pick his way through the debris.

'The place is destroyed,' Fiona said.

'Maybe not,' Duncan said. 'Give me an hour and I'll see if I can drum up some help.'

After he left, the three of them began sifting through the wreckage of the tearoom.

'Duncan's right,' Marcus said, encouragingly. 'Some of this stuff's not too badly damaged. Maybe it's not as bad as it first appeared.'

Kerra went to examine the china. Only a fraction of the cups and saucers had been smashed. As far as she could tell, the tea and coffee-making machines were still intact. But the beautiful walls . . . there was no way this could all be put straight by the morning.

But she'd reckoned without Duncan.

Duncan To The Rescue

Marcus and Fiona were still wading through the wreckage, laying aside disjointed chairs, sweeping up broken glass, and collecting the remnants of shattered crockery, when Kerra looked up, pushing back tendrils of hair from her damp forehead.

'This is hopeless, and you two look shattered. Why don't you get off now? I'll hold the fort here until Duncan gets back.' She lowered her voice. 'Although what he thinks he can do, I've no idea.'

The sound of car engines and slamming of doors made them all look up. The three of them stood, dumbfounded, as Duncan marched in, followed by Kerra and Fiona's dads, Jock McAlpine, and another couple of men he introduced as friends and colleagues from the surgery. Some of them carried tool kits, others had paintbrushes.

Kerra spun round, staring at them all in turn, her brow wrinkled in confusion.

'What's going on?'

Her dad put an arm around her shoulders.

'We're going to sort this, love,' he said, his voice quiet. 'You three have done all you can. Leave it to us now.'

'Your dad's right, Kerra,' Duncan cut in.

'Really, Duncan. It's good of you, but — '

'No buts. Tell her to go home, Mr Morrison.'

'The doctor's right, Kerra. You look all in.' He grinned. 'Besides, your mother's just dying to know what's been going on down here.'

Duncan took her arm and started leading her through the shop to the back yard where her car was parked.

'You, too, sis.' He beckoned Fiona to follow them. 'You ladies have had enough excitement for one day.'

It was midnight when Kerra drove up

the rough farm lane, where she could see the lights of the cottage still burning ahead. The back door flew open as she pulled into the yard and her mother rushed out.

'Oh, Kerra!' She held out her arms and her daughter fell into them. She began examining her face, gently lifting back straying locks of hair, as you would for a child who had fallen and injured herself. 'Are you all right?'

Kerra nodded, close to tears again.

'I'm fine, Mum. You shouldn't have stayed up.'

'Is it bad? Duncan said they had done a lot of damage.'

'Bad enough.' Her daughter's voice sounded hollow. 'We'll have to postpone the opening.' She thought of the cheerful room Marcus had admired only a few short hours ago, and all the hours of graft and sweat she and Fiona had put into getting it just right before the official opening. It was to have been the launch of her new business, the start of her dream. Now it had all been tarnished.

Rosemary Morrison pressed her fingers to her temples.

'I never thought they would do that.' Her words were hardly discernible, but Kerra's head came up.

'Who are you talking about, Mum?' Her eyes were wide. 'Are you saying you know who did this?'

Rosemary's defiant look made her start.

'Of course I do. It was your cousins!'

Kerra stared at her mother.

'Sarah and David? You're not serious!'

Rosemary's eyes narrowed.

'I wouldn't put anything past that pair, especially David. Remember all the threats they made when the will was read? They said they wouldn't let it rest.'

'But through the courts, Mum. They threatened to contest Uncle Sinclair's will through the courts.'

Rosemary sniffed.

'Well, it seems to me that they've found a more instant way of getting back at you.'

Kerra got up and paced the room. It was unthinkable that her cousins could do this to her.

She climbed into bed that night with no hope of sleep, but exhaustion, both mental and physical, took over. The next thing she knew, her mother was in her room, drawing back the curtains, letting the bright morning sunshine flood in. She shook her gently.

'Wake up, Kerra, or you'll miss your opening day.'

'If this is a joke, Mum, then I'm not appreciating it.'

'It's no joke,' her father's voice came from the door. His hair was tousled and he looked tired, but he was smiling. There was a glint of triumph in his eyes.

'Your mum's right. We have an opening to attend, so let's get organised,' he said.

Kerra went through the ritual of showering and putting on the pale green floaty dress she'd chosen specially for the event. But she was feeling like a fraud as she sat in the back of her parents' car as it trundled along the lanes to Craigallen. The tearoom was wrecked, and no amount of good intentions would have put that right in a night.

A crowd had gathered around the door of the tearoom and people turned to wave as the Morrisons' car passed.

'I feel like a celebrity,' Rosemary Morrison chirped, smoothing down the skirt of her new cream linen suit.

'I think it's Kerra they're waiting for,' her husband said.

Thoroughly confused, Kerra stepped out of the car. The crowd parted for her to enter the tearoom. Her eyes widened as she stepped inside.

It looked exactly as it had done before last night's vandals' attack. The tables had been mended, and the pretty gingham covers replaced, the graffiti-daubed walls had been given a restoring coat of cream paint. She sniffed. She could still smell its newness. The crockery had been washed and was stacked in an orderly fashion back on the shelves. Bowls of fresh flowers were everywhere She put a hand to her head. She was shaking.

'I don't understand.'

'All these wonderful people have worked all night to achieve this.' Marcus came forward, his eyes moist. 'You have a lot of friends, little one,' he said, not bothering to hide the emotion in his voice.

Fiona came up and squeezed her arm.

'Can you believe this? Isn't it wonderful, Kerra?'

Amongst the assembled group in the room she could pick out the faces of the men Duncan had brought with him last night. Starting with her father, Kerra hugged each man in turn, finishing with Duncan. She felt his arms come up in response, then he cleared his throat to step back and look round the room.

'What do you think, Kerra? Will it pass muster?

'It's better than that. It's perfect,' she said, her eyes filling with tears.

At her nod, Fiona went to open the door and let the assembled crowd in. There were more people than Kerra expected. Word of the efforts of her friends last night had got round and everyone wanted to be part of the opening celebrations. Even the local paper turned up, who said the story was good enough to put on the front page.

Kerra stood on a chair and made a little speech. She tried not to be too gushing in her thanks, but the people who mattered knew how truly grateful she was. Several times during the course of the morning, Kerra caught Duncan watching her and smiled back across the crowded room. It wasn't until the last guests were leaving that he approached her, handing her a glass of champagne.

'Today's been a triumph.' He waved his own glass around the room. 'The place looks great.'

She followed his gaze.

'Yes, it does. Thanks to you.'

'We only put right what you and

Fiona had already achieved. You should give yourselves a pat on the back.'

She reached up and kissed his cheek, whispering, 'I'll never forget what you did for me.'

He looked down at her, and for a long, lingering moment her heart stood still.

'You look very beautiful, Kerra,' he said softly.

For one brief second, none of her surroundings seemed important. The only thing that mattered was this man, standing close to her, and the grey eyes that held her own. Then he stepped back, and the moment was gone.

Her parents came up behind her.

'We're going off now, love,' her father said. 'Will you be all right for a lift home?'

She'd forgotten she'd come in her parents' car.

'We'll make sure she's not stranded,' Duncan said.

Fraser and Rosemary each kissed their daughter. She hugged them back and returned their waves as they went out the door.

Duncan was still standing beside her.

'Fiona and I are having a bar lunch at the Crofters',' he said. 'Why don't you come with us?'

She'd come back to earth with a thud. Duncan Crombie thought of her as a friend and, whether she liked it or not, that was how it would stay.

* * *

'The best thing about this place,' Duncan said with a cynical grin as they walked into the dining-room of the Crofters' Arms and cast a glance over the empty tables, 'is that you never have to book.'

Fiona gave her brother a nudge.

'I think it's nice,' she whispered.

Kerra sat down, staring out the window. From this position there was an unrestricted view of the tearoom.

Duncan followed her gaze along the street and frowned, wondering if Kerra realised that from this point her tearoom could be kept under full surveillance.

'Are you two going to daydream all day, or are we going to order?' Fiona waved her menu at them. 'I'm starving.'

Her friend's voice cut through Kerra's thoughts, and she gave herself a mental shake.

'Me, too.' She smiled and turned to the menu.

The bottle of sparkling wine Duncan ordered was brought to their table by Murray Glenn himself. He gave the strange little bow he'd done the first time they'd met.

'Ah, the doctor and Miss Morrison. How nice to see you both again.' His appreciative gaze slid from Kerra's face to Fiona's. To Duncan's annoyance, he saw his sister flush. It was all the encouragement Glenn needed.

'I don't think I've met this young lady.' The intimate smile he directed at Fiona made Kerra's toes curl. She daren't look at Duncan; she could feel his hostility from where she sat.

Dragging his eyes away from Fiona's flustered face, Murray inquired, 'Have you made your choices yet, or would you like me to suggest something?

'I think we can manage,' Duncan said curtly.

Murray lifted the wine from its nest of ice and made to pour some into Duncan's glass. Kerra held her breath, hoping he wouldn't antagonise the man by refusing the traditional tasting. But he sat back, allowing Murray to pour the sample. He then drank it and nodded his approval.

'Just leave the bottle. We can do the rest,' he said.

Murray inclined his head and turned to leave, then glanced back, his gaze travelling along the High Street to the tearoom. He turned innocent eyes on them.

'I was sorry to hear about your little incident last night. Did the intruders do much damage?'

Kerra saw Duncan's chest rise as he

struggled to keep his temper. Was he thinking the same thing as her — that Murray Glenn was involved in the attack on the tearoom?

It was Fiona who answered Murray's question.

'My brother came to our rescue.' She smiled, her eyes full of pride. 'The place was wrecked, but he called out the troops and they worked all night to set it straight.' She was gazing at Duncan with something akin to hero worship.

But Duncan was watching Murray, studying his reaction, and Kerra followed his gaze. She thought she saw the man's eyes narrow, his nostrils flare a fraction. But she could have been wrong. Perhaps she was seeing what she wanted to see — some kind of hint that Murray was guilty?

A smiling waitress arrived, order pad in hand. Murray turned on his heel and marched smartly away.

'What a nice man,' Fiona murmured. 'We should have invited him to the opening.'

Kerra shot Duncan a look and saw him frown.

'I thought you were hungry?' He glanced up at the waitress. 'Can you give us a minute? We haven't quite made up our minds yet.'

'Of course, sir,' the girl said. 'I'll come back.'

Duncan glanced at Kerra before turning to his sister.

'Don't you realise that this man is Kerra's strongest competition in this town?'

Fiona shot him an indignant look.

'It doesn't mean he's the enemy, does it?' She smiled, clearly pleased that she'd made such an impression on the handsome hotel owner. 'Why can't we all be friends?'

Duncan's grey eyes were stern, and he leaned across the table to enforce his point, but Kerra touched his arm and shook her head. She now knew that Duncan was as suspicious of Glenn as she was.

An Apology

'You didn't accuse them, Mum?' Kerra's voice rose in horror. 'Please tell me you didn't accuse Sarah and David of trying to destroy the tearoom?'

It was two weeks later, and they were sitting at the breakfast table in the farm cottage, having just downed plates of scrambled eggs and bacon. Rosemary shot her husband an uneasy glance.

Kerra's eyes rolled to the ceiling in a gesture of dismay but before she could speak her mother put up a hand as though in defence.

'All right, I was wrong,' she said. 'I should never have contacted Sarah, but I was just so angry that anyone especially a member of our own family — could do such a thing to you.' She gave her daughter a beseeching look. 'But I never actually accused them. I just asked if they knew anything about what had happened.'

'And?' Kerra asked, her eyes wide with disbelief.

'Well they denied it, of course. At least Sarah did. I never spoke to David.' She lifted her cup and realising it was empty, put it back on the table. 'She seemed shocked.'

'Not as shocked as I am,' Kerra said.

'Don't blame your mother. She was just looking after your interests, love,' her father said gently. 'Anyway, there was no harm done, because Sarah apologised for her behaviour in the solicitor's office that day. I think she and David have finally accepted the fact that Sinclair left the business to you.'

Her mother was nodding in agreement.

'I am sorry, Kerra. I know I shouldn't have interfered.'

There was such a look of remorse in her mother's eyes that Kerra was now feeling like the guilty one. Moving quickly to her mother's side and putting her arms around her, she said, 'It's me who should be apologising. I know you were just looking out for me.'

'Right, now that's sorted,' her father said, picking up his discarded newspaper again and shaking out the pages, 'who's for another cup of tea?'

Kerra chastised herself as she drove into Craigallen an hour later. She knew her mother had had the best of intentions, but she couldn't help wondering how her cousins really felt. She wasn't sure she believed they no longer blamed her for getting the legacy they had been so certain was coming to them. Their venom towards her at the reading of the will had been real enough.

Could they have heard that the business was now almost sold? Maybe they'd make another bid for a share of the proceeds? They couldn't know she had already used a quarter of the money to set up trust funds for their children. The only other person aware of that was Matthew West, and he certainly wouldn't have told them.

She drove past the tearoom and turned along the lane to the rear parking area. Two weeks ago she had stood with Fiona amongst the wreckage of her business, believing her dreams had been shattered. Who would have thought the vandals had done them a favour? In their own venomous way they had given Kerra's Catering an amazing boost.

The journalist from the 'Gazette' had, as promised, made sure the story got the front page. The way Duncan had rallied their friends and family to work all through night and put the smashed tearoom to rights had touched everyone and orders were now pouring in for Kerra to supply the food at a string of local events.

Her assistants, Will, and Janie Campbell, a shy eighteen-year-old, the daughter of a friend of Kerra's mother, were already in the kitchen when she arrived and had made a start on preparations for the buffet lunch at Blairdhu House. The old property had recently been bought by

London couple Lauren and Harry King, who were running it as a corporate events' venue. The current function involved a Murder Mystery Weekend, where the participants had to follow a series of clues to help each other reveal the culprit.

She wasn't sure how that would help them to 'bond', but that wasn't her problem. She had a contract to supply a quality buffet lunch for 25 people, and if the Kings liked what she supplied, they had promised future business.

She was taking a tray of vol-au-vents out of the oven when Fiona's bright head appeared round the door.

'Someone out front to see you, Kerra,' she called.

Kerra slipped the heavy tray onto the table and pushed back a stray lock of hair with the back of her hand.

'Now's not a good time. Who is it?'

Fiona grimaced and lowered her voice.

'I think you better come.'

'You attend your visitor, Kerra,' Will

146

called from the back of the kitchen. 'I'll finish off the fillings for these.'

Kerra shot him a grateful look and, ripping off her apron, went through to the tearoom. She was pleased to see it was busy. Fiona was extracting a cream cake from the glass case — a tricky operation using the silver tongs.

She nodded to the table by the window. Kerra froze for a second. The woman sitting with her back to her, her gaze fixed on the street outside, was her cousin, Sarah. She took a deep breath, glancing across to Fiona, who raised her shoulders. It all looked quiet enough. Perhaps Sarah hadn't come to cause trouble after all. She fixed a smile on her face and walked to her cousin's table.

'Sarah! How nice to see you.' The whole of that morning's conversation with her mother flashed through her head. But she'd said she hadn't actually accused Sarah and David of the vandal attack. But why else would she be here other than to complain? She sat down.

147

Sarah's eyes now slid over the tearoom.

'Is this the place they trashed?'

Kerra nodded.

'It wasn't us, you know. I know your mother doesn't believe it, but David and I had nothing to do with that.' She lifted the teapot, pulling over a second cup and saucer on the table. 'And I'm speaking for both of us.' She inclined her head to indicate her surroundings. 'Is this what your inheritance bought?'

'Partly,' Kerra said stiffly. Surely her cousin wasn't going to make a scene in here? 'Look, Sarah, I'm a bit pushed for time just at the minute.'

'Then I'll come to the point,' Sarah said. 'I owe you an apology.' She bit her lip. 'I can't imagine what came over me in Matthew West's office that day. I should never have said all those hurtful things, and neither should David.'

Kerra took the tea she'd pushed towards her.

'It's all water under the bridge now, Sarah. I know what a shock it must have been.' She stopped herself from going any further. 'Let's just agree to forget it,' she said.

'No, your mother was right to chastise me. It made me realise how awful we've been to you. But I need to know you believe me when I say that neither David nor I had anything to do with vandalising this place.' She met Kerra's eyes and it was obvious she was telling the truth. 'Oh, don't get me wrong. We're no angels, as I suspect you already know, but we would never do anything like that.'

But that was the thing. If her cousins weren't responsible for the damage, then who was? She felt a shiver run through her. Fiona's father had suggested it could have been some kind of misguided prank. She'd reported it to the police after the opening day, and they came to examine the smashed lock on the back door, but apart from suggesting that it could have been a professional job, made to look opportunist, any evidence that might have

149

been left disappeared when Duncan organised her family and friends to put the mess right.

If the police were right, and the vandals had been some kind of professional criminals, then it put a whole new slant on things. They must have known there would be no money on the premises.

Her mind kept returning to Murray Glenn. Had that been venom she'd seen in his eyes when Fiona told so gleefully how Duncan had foiled the vandals' attempt to destroy her business before it had even got off the ground?

'You do believe me, don't you, Kerra?' Sarah's voice cut into her thoughts, making her start.

She stood up, touching her cousin's shoulder as she moved behind her chair.

'Of course I do, Sarah.'

'Can we forget all the stuff we said about the will?'

'Consider it forgotten.' Kerra smiled, glancing at the clock. 'I'm really sorry, but we're catering for quite an important event in less than and hour . . . '

'You get off.' Sarah smiled, rising from the table. 'I'll give you a call. Maybe we can meet in Inverness and have lunch one day.'

'That would be lovely.' Kerra smiled back before turning towards the kitchen again.

'I forgot to say,' Sarah called after her. 'I love what you've done with the tearoom.'

Kerra turned, surprised, and glanced across at Fiona, who was beaming at both of them.

'Thanks, Sarah. I appreciate that.'

'We're all sorted.' Will grinned, indicating the large bowl of diced chicken breast in its creamy white sauce. 'Will this be enough for the fillings?'

Kerra patted his shoulder.

'It looks perfect. We'll make the vol-au-vents up on site.' She flashed another look at the kitchen clock. 'We have to get a move on, so let's start

151

loading the van.'

Janie had been busy organising the crockery, glasses and cutlery they would take with them, and all three began packing them into boxes before loading them into the back of the second-hand van Kerra had recently bought. It was now a smart dark green colour, with Kerra's Catering in huge white lettering on either side. Last to go in would be the food. This type of event was a first for all of them, and she was determined to pull out all the stops to make sure it went without a hitch.

Blairdhu House was less than three miles from Craigallen, and she could sense the excitement of the other two as they drove up the curving drive to park in a previously arranged spot at the back door.

Will let out a low whistle.

'I'd heard this place was something special, but I wasn't expecting this. It's massive!'

Kerra nodded, taking a second to sweep her eyes over the grounds. Even here at the back of the once-grand stone house, the sense of space was awesome. One or two of the trees looked as though they needed attention, where some of the wind-damaged branches hung precariously low. It didn't take long to realise that the first impression of grandeur had to be tempered by the fact that, in places, the house was crumbling.

Paint peeled from doors and there were window frames that needed attention. Kerra found herself wondering what condition the roof was in, let alone the bedrooms the Kings' corporate guests would be occupying.

Kerra had been shown round on her first visit by Lauren King, but at the time she'd been more interested in what facilities the large kitchen had to offer to pay much attention to the woman. She vaguely remembered an elegant figure, fashionable heels that clicked on the stone floors, and a pair of calculating green eyes. Mrs King would be demanding perfection.

She turned her thoughts back to the kitchen and, with a sigh, remembered that facilities here were basic. Brass taps over the sink were stubborn to yield and she was glad she hadn't relied on using the ancient Aga, which could have come straight from a museum. Squinting across to the fridge she wasn't sure she believed Lauren King's assurance that it would be adequate. In future, when she inspected prospective events' venues, she would be more thorough in checking out the kitchen facilities.

A quick clicking of heels on the flagged passage outside alerted them to the approach of their employer for the day. Lauren King arrived, trailing two young women, dressed like maids, in black dresses and white aprons.

'This is Heidi and Emma. They're going to help you,' she announced. 'Just tell them what's needed.'

Heidi and Emma turned out to be part-time staff at the house, who had been drafted in to help out at such events.

Kerra's Catering had been contracted to supply only one buffet lunch, although she knew the guests had arrived the previous night and were staying until the next morning.

'Mrs King and a woman from the village are doing the breakfasts and suppers between them,' Heidi explained.

Emma giggled.

'If that's what you'd like to call it.'

Kerra raised an eyebrow, not sure she wanted to hear this. But Heidi, now enjoying her platform, continued.

'Well, you hear things, don't you? When you're polishing and sweeping.' She lowered her voice and brought her face closer, as though to share a secret. 'I've heard some of the guests talking and they've been saying the meals are awful.'

Kerra's heart sank. She'd been hoping this would be the first of many events that would require her services at Blairdhu House. But if what this girl said was true, event organisers might be giving this place a wide berth in future. She sighed.

'We have work to do. Let's just get on with it.'

The crisp green linen and matching paper napkins looked good on the trestle table Lauren King had provided. Heidi and Emma had been entrusted with clean-up duties in the kitchen, while Kerra, Will and Janie, served the guests. As far as she could tell from the approving looks and snatches of overheard conversation, the IT people were enjoying the buffet. Quite a few came over to compliment her on the wonderful food. It was with a sigh of satisfaction that she later helped the others to clear up.

She was stacking dishes on a worktop when she heard a tremendous crack and then a scream. Rushing to the back door, she was just in time to see one of the young female guests attempt to jump clear as a hefty branch from one of the damaged chestnut trees she'd noticed earlier came crashing down.

But the girl hadn't been quick enough, and the branch caught her a glancing blow on the shoulder Kerra stared, horrified, as the girl crumpled to the ground.

She was still prostrate on the grass when Kerra and the others got to her, an angry red bruise on her bare arm. A man was on his knees beside the young woman, rubbing her hands, calling her name.

'Shona! Shona!' He looked back frantically. 'Somebody call an ambulance!'

But another member of the IT group was already on his mobile, punching in 999.

The man at the injured girl's side was looking round desperately again.

Kerra rushed to join him on his knees. Touching the girl's forehead, her eyes flickered.

'I don't think she's unconscious,' she said, reaching for her phone. Duncan answered immediately.

'Kerra?' he asked worriedly.

Kerra quickly described the situation, explaining that an ambulance was on its way, but until it arrived they needed immediate advice on how to help the girl. The sound of his voice, calm and professional, was giving Kerra confidence as he issued instructions.

'Just a minute, Duncan.' She flicked her phone to loudspeaker to free her hands.

His voice at the other end of the phone continued in the same calm, encouraging tones.

'Make sure nothing is obstructing her airway and that she's breathing easily. Put her in the recovery position on her side. I'm on my way.'

She'd followed Duncan's instructions to the letter and now sat back on her heels, looking around the circle of anxious faces.

'I'm sure your friend will be fine,' she said weakly.

There was a call from behind, and Lauren King pushed her way to the front to stand, horrified, staring down at the girl's still frame.

'Has anybody called an ambulance?'

Kerra nodded.

'Of course,' Lauren said. 'Is there anything I can do?'

'We've spoken to a doctor and followed his advice. The ambulance shouldn't be long.' Kerra tried to sound reassuring. She bit her lip and squinted along the drive. Where was the ambulance? Where was Duncan? The thought had no sooner raced through her head than the familiar little red sports car sped up the drive, its tyres throwing up a dust storm as it screeched to a standstill.

Duncan, medical bag in hand, was running towards them. He nodded to Kerra and squatted down beside the injured girl, who had now begun to cry softly. Everything seemed to be happening at once. Behind them an ambulance was squealing to a halt, there was a slamming of doors, and the sound of running feet, and two paramedics, backpacks bulging with medical equipment, raced up. One of them was carrying a folded stretcher. Duncan got up and stood aside.

He nodded around the assembled crowd.

'She'll be fine — '

But before he had finished the sentence, his face froze. Kerra saw the colour drain from his handsome face. Confused, she followed the direction of his gaze. He was staring at Lauren King! She heard him clear his throat in an attempt to compose himself. He nodded wordlessly at the woman.

She smiled, her green eyes sparkling. 'Hello, Duncan.'

For a split second their eyes locked and Kerra felt she was intruding on a moment of such intimacy that a shiver ran down her spine. They knew each other. And from what she could see, they'd been more than just friends.

He was walking towards Kerra on his way back to his car and touched her arm as he passed.

'She's in good hands now. I'm sure she'll be fine.'

But his usually animated face now lacked expression. She was tempted to follow him, ask if he was all right, but the sight of Lauren King, staring after him, a look of triumph in the lovely eyes, tore a lump out of Kerra's heart.

A Serious Matter

Kerra woke next morning with a thumping headache. She'd hardly slept. All she wanted to do now was pull the duvet over her head and forget the world, but there was a business to run. People were depending on her.

The corporate event had been a minor triumph, and Lauren had told her there would more in the pipeline, if she was interested. She should be feeling on top of the world, but she wasn't. The look that had flashed between Lauren and Duncan was running circles around her mind. Had they had an affair? Lauren was married and Kerra didn't think it would be Duncan's style to have an affair with a married woman. It was something else.

She pressed her fingertips against her temples, feeling the throb. None of this was any of her business. It wasn't as if she was in a relationship with Duncan. They were friends and that was all.

Kerra dragged herself out of bed and into the shower. By the time she got out, dried her hair and dressed, she was feeling marginally better.

The first scattering of cottages on the approach to Craigallen were just ahead, but as she drove along the familiar quiet country road, something caught her eye.

It was a dark car, parked by a farm gate along one of the area's many lanes. She saw two people in the front seats. Perhaps they had broken down and she wondered briefly if she should offer help, but something stopped her. The couple hadn't looked as if they were in any kind of trouble. Then she saw their heads coming together. They were kissing! She smiled, thankful she hadn't barged in on them. At least some people's love lives were on track.

She was first to arrive and let herself into the kitchen, glancing with approval at the line of ovens, fridge and sinks. For the umpteenth time she reminded herself that this business was what she had to concentrate on.

She slipped off her jacket, then went through to the tearoom. It was the calm before the storm. She wandered around the room, trailing a hand over the tables. The tearoom was rapidly becoming a great success — something she and Fiona could be proud of.

She jumped when Fiona came up behind her.

'Everything all right, Kerra?' She was already in the dark green uniform they all wore.

'Of course, why wouldn't it be?' The words came out sharper than she'd intended, and she saw the girl's eyebrows go up. 'Sorry. I didn't mean to bite your head off. Everything's fine. I was just having a look around.' Then she looked up, smiling. 'This place is doing really well, Fiona. You should be proud of yourself.'

Fiona raised a hand in mock salute.

'Just doing my job, ma'am.' She laughed.

Kerra could see she'd been pleased at the compliment. She made a note to praise all her staff a bit more often.

Work was now coming in at such a rate that the three of them in the kitchen were struggling to cope. Kerra went back to the notes she'd taken at the initial interviews. She'd made a list of some of the other candidates who'd turned up that day and ran a finger down the list of the others she'd thought might be suitable, making a mental note to contact them. The current order was for an anniversary buffet, which she, Will and Janie were preparing, when Duncan stuck his head round the door from the tearoom.

He raised his voice above the noise of the whirring mixer she was using.

'Got a minute, Kerra?'

His unexpected appearance sent her heart into an alarming somersault. She switched off the machine, stopping to take a deep, steadying breath, before following him back through. Surely he hadn't come to explain about Lauren? But then, why would he? It was none of her business, after all.

He'd gone over to a table that had been set with a pot of tea, two cups and saucers, plus a plate of the tearoom's freshly baked scones. He looked up as she walked towards him and smiled, indicating the things on the table.

'I took the liberty of ordering us some tea.'

She wanted to smile back, thank him and collapse gratefully into the chair opposite, but she frowned.

'No patients today, Doctor?'

He looked up, not sure if she was joking. She sat down.

'I am quite busy, Duncan. Was it something important?'

He was embarrassed now.

'It's my morning off, actually, and I'm here to put some work your way,' he said stiffly. 'There's a big farm sale coming up and I thought you might want to bid for the catering contract, but if you want me to leave . . . '

She coloured, ashamed that she'd spoken so sharply.

'I'm sorry, Duncan. I didn't mean to snap at you like that.' She smiled, reaching for the teapot and pouring them both a cup. 'All this was really thoughtful. I could do with the break.' She forced herself to meet his eyes. 'Now, tell me about this farm sale.'

As he spoke, his face became animated.

'All the big farmers will be there. It could be a great vehicle to promote your catering business, Kerra.'

She was touched by his enthusiasm to help, but what did she expect? He was a caring man. She remembered how he'd rushed to Blairdhu House that day to help the injured girl, but then maybe he'd had an ulterior motive. No, his shock at seeing Lauren King there had been real enough.

'Any update on the girl who got injured at Blairdhu House?' she asked, keeping her voice light.

He nodded.

'It looked worse than it was. I rang the hospital and they were satisfied that she was well enough to go home.'

Out of the corner of her eye she saw the tearoom door open and Murray Glenn come in. Duncan had followed her glance and the corners of his mouth turned down.

'He hangs around here quite a lot now, doesn't he?' he said with obvious distaste.

It was a second before Kerra answered. She was thinking the same thing. She was also remembering that Murray drove a dark car, and it had been a dark car she'd seen earlier that morning with the kissing couple in the front. She pressed her lips hard together. Fiona and Murray? She hoped not.

* * *

The anniversary buffet was an evening event, but the preparations for it had

168

been completed by mid-afternoon, so Kerra suggested that Will and Janie should go home for a few hours. She'd contacted the agents responsible for the farm sale and was given details of the clients' requirements for the catering.

Gathering her menus, recipe books and notebooks around her, she spent the next hour working out quantities for the expected numbers, costing ingredients, and estimating a price. She knew she was cutting her profits to the bone, but Duncan had been right. If she got this contract it could be pivotal in the success of her business.

Fiona was putting the finishing touches to closing the tearoom when Kerra looked in to say she was leaving.

'Duncan told me about the farm sale. It would be a good contract to get, wouldn't it?'

Kerra nodded.

'It would. It was nice of him to think of me.' She'd been so busy all day she hadn't had time to brood on how upset she'd been at the look he'd shared with

Lauren. She forced herself to concentrate on the job in hand.

She had planned to go home, have a meal with her parents, a shower, and be back here by six, but glancing at her watch now she realised there was no time for that. She'd make herself a sandwich here and give her face a quick splash. But she did need to clear her head, and a walk in the countryside around Craigallen would do the trick.

She went out to the car park. The only car in the yard was her own. Where was Fiona's car? She half turned to go back and offer her friend a lift home, but something stopped her. Murray Glenn did seem to be haunting the tearoom these days. Kerra had vaguely imagined he was checking out the competition, but now she wasn't so sure.

She got into the car and drove out of the car park. She wondered if Fiona would be watching her. She made the usual left turn for home, but this time she cut back, parking in a side road from where she could see the access to their car park along the side of the tearoom. She sat there for a few minutes until guilt consumed her. She was spying on Fiona! What kind of friend did that make her?

Kerra was reaching for the ignition key when she saw the black car approach and turn down the lane, reappearing two minutes later with Fiona in the passenger seat. This time she got a good view of the driver as the car purred along the High Street. It was Murray Glenn.

Should she approach her, warn her what kind of man Murray Glenn really was? She sighed. Fiona probably wouldn't listen, and she might jeopardise their friendship if she started poking her nose into what was none of her business. But she couldn't just sit back and do nothing.

The anniversary party went with a swing, and because they had been so well prepared there were no hitches. She couldn't believe they had catered for 70 people, as well as having to work from a marquee.

Rona and Becky, the two new members of the team Kerra had selected from her list, proved to be hard workers, and fitted right in. She'd been particularly impressed with Becky. She'd given no indication at the initial interview that she had worked in a commercial kitchen before, but she obviously had.

She'd finished her costings for the farm sale. Eagleton Farm was one of the biggest this side of Inverness and she'd been warned that it was to be a high profile auction with hundreds of bidders coming from all over the country to purchase farm equipment. Many of them would be expecting a high-quality buffet, and Kerra and her team would be supplying smoked salmon sandwiches, filled bridge rolls, plus elegant, tiny cakes and pastries.

The agent had insisted on a sealed bid, which had to be in his hands by the next morning, and the only way Kerra could do that was to deliver it in person to his Inverness office. As she took the quiet country road, past familiar crofts, whose owners were all friends of her parents, Kerra's thoughts drifted back to Fiona.

Lots of things were now falling into place. She remembered a certain spring to the girl's step, an excited gleam in her eyes. She'd briefly wondered at the time if there was a new boyfriend on the scene, but when she didn't mention anything, Kerra assumed her imagination had been working overtime. Now she realised that all the clues had been there, if only she hadn't been too busy to take them seriously.

It was the secrecy that disturbed Kerra most. Murray Glenn knew his relationship with Fiona would not meet with her brother's approval. She slapped the steering wheel. That was it! She must tell Duncan. He'd know what to do.

It was four o'clock next day when the agent rang to tell Kerra she had the contract for the farm sale, but since it was less than a week away — and they had other orders to deal with in the meantime — it was all hands to the pump. Rona and Becky had been drafted in again to help.

The kitchen was so busy now that Kerra didn't have time to worry about Fiona's new romance, but she didn't miss the fact that Murray was now coming into the tearoom on a daily basis. Short of banning him from the premises, there wasn't anything she could do about it.

When utensils started to go missing in the kitchen Kerra was prepared to give everyone the benefit of the doubt. They were busy, after all, and items were probably just being put away in the wrong places. But it slowed things up, and it shouldn't be happening.

Mistakes over orders were a more serious matter. The first time it happened, Kerra was annoyed. The order was for a children's birthday party. When she went to load the van, there was only one tray of sandwiches in the fridge, instead of the two she was certain had been made — and where were the trifles? All she could see was a container of fresh fruit salad and some made-up jellies.

When she tackled Will about it he shrugged his shoulders and gave her a confused look.

'The order said fruit and jellies, there was nothing about trifles.' He reached for the order form. 'See for yourself.'

She took the slip of paper from him, frowning at the scrawled words. He was right. There was no mention of trifles. But she'd taken that order herself and written it down. It certainly looked like her writing.

'Sorry, Will,' she said with a deep sigh. 'It's not your fault.' But she knew she had not made a mistake. Something was going on here and she was determined to get to the bottom of it.

It was the Friday before the farm sale and the fridges in the kitchen were packed with the efforts of the previous days' labour. Deciding she would need only Will and Janie at the sale, Kerra gave Rona and Becky their wages for the week and thanked them for their efforts, then wished them goodnight as they all trooped out the back door.

Kerra went through to the tearoom.

'I feel like a stranger in here.' She laughed. 'We've been so busy I've hardly seen you.'

'You have all been looking a bit up to your eyes in it lately,' Fiona called back as she locked the till.

'I haven't even seen you in our domain lately.' Kerra made a weak attempt at humour.

'Oh, I've been in and out of the kitchen, but you were all too busy to notice,' Fiona said, flashing her brilliant smile.

Not for the first time, Kerra realised just what a really pretty girl her friend was.

'You're chirpy tonight,' she said cautiously. 'Big date?'

Fiona pursed her lips and sighed happily.

'The biggest,' she said, glancing at the clock. 'And I'm already late. You don't mind if I fly off, do you, Kerra?'

Kerra shook her head, wearily. She was in no position to mind. She had an early start in the morning to make the mountain of sandwiches that would be needed. The fillings had all been prepared in advance, so it shouldn't take them more than an hour or so.

It was just after five when she set off for home. She still hadn't approached Duncan about his sister's friendship with Murray. She knew that he had no higher regard for the man than she did. But there was something more bothering her tonight. The incidents that had been plaguing her work over the past week had been irritating, but surely not malicious? So why did that phrase 'I've been in and out of the kitchen, but you were all too busy to notice' keep running through her head?

Something clicked in her mind and she rammed on the brakes, turning the car in the direction of the Health Centre.

'Watch Your Step'

The waiting-room was empty when Kerra walked in. The receptionist glanced away from her screen.

'I'm sorry, surgery's finished for the day. If you'd like to make an appointment — '

'Mrs . . . ' Kerra racked her brain for the name of the woman Duncan had introduced her to that first night at the Crofters' Arms. Then it clicked. 'Mrs Faulds, isn't it?'

Eileen Faulds looked up and Kerra saw the recognition in her eyes.

'Oh, it's you, Miss Morrison.'

'Kerra, please.' She smiled.

'Have you come to see the doctor?' She glanced up at the clock. 'He's about finished.'

At that very moment Duncan himself appeared, carrying a pile of cards, which Kerra assumed were his patients' records. He gave her a surprised smile as he headed for the reception desk and handed the cards to Eileen Faulds.

The sight of him coming towards her made Kerra's heart somersault. She focused on steadying her breathing, reminding herself she was here on Fiona's behalf.

'I take it this isn't an official call?' He jerked his head back towards his examination room and gave her a quizzical grin.

She felt the colour rush to her cheeks and looked away.

'Of course not,' she said. 'I need to speak to you.'

She saw the flicker of concern cross his face and glanced back to see Elaine had gone back to her computer.

'It's about Fiona,' she said quietly.

He took her arm and, calling goodnight to his receptionist, quickly walked Kerra towards the door. In the car park he opened the passenger door of his car for her to get in, then went round to climb into the driver's side.

'OK,' he said, turning to her. 'What's this about?'

She took a deep breath.

'I hope I'm doing the right thing here.'

'Yes?' he said encouragingly.

'I won't beat about the bush. Fiona is seeing Murray Glenn.' The words came out in a rush and she glanced up at him, trying to gauge a reaction. He turned to stare at her.

'Are you sure?'

Kerra repeated what she'd seen, every word sounding like a betrayal of her friend. She sighed.

'I can't think of any other explanation of why they would be together. Maybe I shouldn't be telling you all this. It is Fiona's business after all. It's just that I'm so worried about her. Murray Glenn is a skunk.'

Duncan looked up quickly.

'A skunk?'

Kerra nodded, remembering the time he had called at the kitchen when the others had gone home for the night. He'd no doubt thought she would be easy prey, flattered that he was prepared to go to this trouble to persuade her to have dinner with him. But the way he eyed her had made her blood run cold, so she'd bundled him out, leaving him in no doubt that she wouldn't be accepting the invitation.

'He tried the same thing with me. I told him I wasn't interested. But Fiona . . . ' Her shoulders rose in a hopeless shrug. 'Well, it looks like she's fallen for his line.'

Duncan nodded, his face serious.

'You were right to warn me. Something has to be done.'

She looked away, her teeth catching her bottom lip.

'Don't tell me there's more?' he asked anxiously.

Kerra paused, choosing her words carefully.

'I'm not sure. It's just that . . . ' She met his eyes, and the concern she saw there made her want to reach out to him. 'We've been having these incidents in the kitchen.'

'What kind of incidents?'

'Oh, nothing serious. It's just that . . . ' She hesitated not sure she should be saying this. 'Well, someone might be trying to sabotage the business.'

Duncan stared at her.

'Sabotage? That doesn't make sense. Who would do that?'

'Murray Glenn might. We've won a few good contracts lately, and then there is this farm sale job.'

His eyebrows shot up.

'Wait a minute! You're suggesting Fiona's got something to do with this? I know she's young, but she's not daft enough to sabotage the business. She's part if it, for goodness' sake!'

'Calm down, Duncan. I'm not suggesting anything of the kind. But we both know Murray Glenn can be manipulative.'

'So?'

'Well, if he's been staging these little 'happenings' with the intention of pointing the finger at Fiona, it could all make sense.'

He was staring at her with such a look of incredulity that she smiled.

'Don't you see? We operate on a basis of trust. If Murray can make us suspicious of each other then he's attacking the very heart of the business.'

'You think that's what he's doing?'

Kerra was remembering how Fiona's comment about being in and out of the kitchen and not being noticed had stuck in her mind. Perhaps that was Murray's plan — to make them suspicious of every innocent remark. It had almost worked — but not quite.

'I think that's exactly what he's doing,' Kerra said.

'Right, that's it. I'm going to put a stop to this.'

Kerra stared at him in alarm.

'You're not going to tackle her?'

But Duncan's hand went up, silencing her.

'I'll be tactful,' he said.

'I won't mention your theory if that's what you're worried about — not yet, anyway.'

She hoped he meant that, but she wasn't confident.

'What time does she arrive in the morning?'

Kerra told him.

'I'll be there to meet her,' he said quietly, turning to her. 'Now, what about a drink? I think we could both use one.'

He'd started the engine before she had a chance to refuse. They drove through the village, passing his parents' farm, where Fiona was no doubt getting ready at that very moment for her date with Murray.

'Nobody ever comes here, so we can have a drink in peace,' he said, pulling into the car park of the Ram's Head.

It was pleasant to sit with him in the relaxing atmosphere of the quiet country pub. After the week she'd just been through, she was beginning to think she'd never experience another calm moment in her life. But here she was, at Duncan's side, resting her head on the back of the comfy old leather bench.

'You look all in,' he said gently, smiling down at her.

His eyes on her like that gave her a warm glow. She wondered if he had ever looked at Lauren King like that? Now that the thought had come into her head she couldn't get rid of it. Should she ask him how he knew her?

She lifted her glass and drank a mouthful of wine.

'Lauren King's offered us some more work supplying buffets for her corporate events.'

She felt rather than saw him stiffen. He put down his glass and she could see the muscles in his jaw working. For a few seconds he said nothing.

'What else is in the pipeline?'

'What?' she asked.

'Well, your business seems to be on the up and up.'

She met his eyes and found no evidence that he was about to bare his soul to her. He'd practically ignored her mention of Lauren King. It couldn't have been plainer. It was none of her business.

Kerra was first to arrive at work next day, but since it was only six a.m. that was hardly surprising. It was the day of the farm sale and there was still plenty to do before they could set off. By the time Will and Janie arrived half an hour later, she'd already made a start on the sandwiches. She wished she could calm this edgy feeling that something bad was about to happen. She hoped she was wrong.

Her eyes kept straying to the clock. Fiona was due to arrive at eight. The tearoom was always busy on Saturdays. There was still ten minutes to go. She wondered if Duncan was already outside? He'd planned to get here before his sister. By Kerra's reckoning that would be any time now.

The soft tap on the door made her jump and when she opened it with shaking hands, Duncan was there, his face grim. She stepped back, allowing him to pass. Out of the corner of her eye she saw a look pass between the other two as she led the way into the deserted tearoom.

She saw Duncan take a deep breath and touched his arm.

'You won't upset her, will you?'

'That's not why I'm here, Kerra,' he said stiffly. 'Fiona's my little sister, and I have to look out for her.'

'Exactly.' Kerra tried to smile. She wished she didn't have this feeling that they were ganging up on the unsuspecting Fiona.

They both heard the back door slam, signalling her friend's arrival.

'I'll leave you to it,' she said, going back to the kitchen.

Fiona was hanging her denim jacket in the tiny cloakroom area and turned to face Kerra.

'I thought I saw Duncan's car out front. Is he here?'

Kerra nodded towards the door.

'He's been waiting for you.'

Fiona gave her a quizzical stare and went into the tearoom.

Will and Janie had started to load up the van and hadn't heard the raised voices. But Kerra had, and she winced. This was all her fault. She should never have mentioned anything to Duncan. It was Fiona's life and they were both interfering. She pressed her fingertips hard against her temples. What had she done?

Kerra heard the front door of the tearoom slam. Duncan must have gone out that way. By the sound of things, the meeting hadn't gone well. She took a deep breath, following the noisy rattling of crockery and banging of cupboard doors, she went into the tearoom.

Fiona wheeled round, her face scarlet with rage.

'I suppose you know all about this?' she accused. She banged some more plates onto the shelves behind the counter and Kerra winced in anticipation of the whole lot crashing to the floor.

'Duncan was only trying to help.' She

hesitated. 'We both think you might be heading for trouble with Murray.'

Fiona glared at her.

'Oh, for heaven's sake, Fiona. We only want to help.'

'Is that what Duncan told you? He didn't mention then that he's full of spite?'

Kerra stared at her, shocked.

'Duncan's not spiteful. He's just looking out for you.'

But Fiona rounded on her.

'Duncan is just plain jealous because his own relationship went pear-shaped.' Her eyes widened. 'I can see he didn't tell you about that. Well, the reason he went to Africa was because he was jilted.'

Kerra's hands flew to her face. She didn't want to hear.

'Lauren Peterson, or King, whatever she calls herself now.' Fiona's hand flew about in a wild gesture. 'She jilted him and broke his heart! And now she's back with a husband in tow — and Duncan is more bitter than ever. That's the reason he's having a go at me. He's jealous!'

Was she hearing right? Lauren King and Duncan? It all fitted. Kerra sank onto a chair.

'Oh, Fiona. Did you say all this to him?'

For the first time since she'd got there, Fiona was looking out of her depth. Her bottom lip quivered and her face crumpled as the tears began to flow. Kerra hurried across the room and put her arms round the stricken girl.

'This is all Murray Glenn's fault,' she muttered.

'Murray loves me,' Fiona whimpered. 'Why does no-one want us to be happy?'

Kerra cradled the sobbing girl until her crying stopped. She stroked her hair.

'We are on your side, you know,' she said gently. 'All I'm saying is be careful. The man is much older than you.'

'I'm twenty-one,' Fiona said defiantly. 'Old enough, I think, to know my own mind.'

'Just watch your step, that's all I'm saying.'

Fiona's lips pursed into a determined pout, but she'd calmed down. She looked at Kerra through wet lashes.

'I can't believe I said all that to Duncan. He'll be so hurt.' She sniffed. 'And now that awful woman is back.'

'I suppose we're talking about the Mrs King who booked us to cater for her murder weekend?'

Fiona nodded.

'I didn't say anything at the time because I thought it was all in the past — and it probably is for her, but I doubt if Duncan sees it that way.'

She remembered the look that passed between them and thought miserably that Fiona was probably right.

'I didn't realise Lauren King used to live here. I don't remember her. I thought she was from London.'

'She is, but she was here for a couple of years, living with her parents over at Fendom Farm.' She glanced up at Kerra. 'You would have been in

Glasgow at the time.'

'The Lauren King I saw didn't look like she'd come from a farming family,' Kerra said flatly.

'Oh, the Petersons weren't farmers; they just lived in the big house. But they didn't stay long before they went back to London. But it was long enough for Lauren to work her poison on Duncan. They were engaged, would you believe? Then she waltzed off back to London, saying she couldn't live in the country.' She shrugged. 'Too quiet for her, apparently. She and Duncan had been going out for about a year when she ditched him.'

Fiona looked up and met Kerra's eyes.

'He was besotted with her, and now that she's back the whole thing is going to start again. I just know it.'

'But Lauren is married now,' Kerra said.

'Have you seen the husband? Seems to me he's conveniently still down in London.'

Kerra bit her lip. Maybe Fiona was right. She'd certainly never met Mr King. She was remembering Lauren's cool green-eyed gaze, the burnished copper hair, and the woman's shapely body. Any man would be entranced.

She felt abandoned. Was her heart to be ripped apart? If so, then she didn't think she could bear it.

Fiona's voice cut into her thoughts.

'Will you talk to Duncan for me, Kerra? I know I spoke out of turn, but he made me so angry.' She searched her friend's face for confirmation she would help. 'I went much too far, it's no wonder that he stormed off in a rage, but I'm really beginning to worry about him.'

Meals On Wheels

Kerra should have been concentrating on making the day ahead a triumph, but as she drove with Will and Janie to Eagleton Farm she couldn't get Fiona's words out of her head. If she was right about Duncan's feelings for Lauren then she wasn't the only one worrying about him.

The farmyard was buzzing as they drove in. A marshall wearing a green armband directed them to the marquee where they were to set up the catering equipment.

'The people for the bar are already here,' he informed them, nodding towards the catering tent.

Eagleton Farm was more estate than farm, so it stood to reason there would be a huge amount of equipment for the auctioneers to sell. But their eyes widened as they picked their way through the melée of activity.

Will gave a low whistle.

'I know Eagleton's a big concern,' he said, 'but I wasn't expecting this kind of operation.'

Farm machinery of all shapes and sizes had been set out in rows in one of the fields, each item displaying its auction number. Smaller pieces of equipment had been grouped into sections and laid out on the grass.

Kerra drove the van round to the back of the marquee and joined the others to check out the available space inside. A very professional-looking bar had been set up at the far side. There was even a bank of optics, and a familiar figure putting the finishing touches to it.

'Murray Glenn!' She froze. Why did it have to be him?

'Isn't that the chap from the Crofters' Arms?' Janie asked. 'Oh, look, he's coming over.'

Not only was he approaching, but he was smiling, his eyes sweeping over each of them until they settled on Kerra. She was immediately on her guard. He would hardly have been delighted to see her team here today.

He came forward, his hand extended, and Kerra accepted his limp greeting. What did Fiona see in this man? Beyond the handsome face, the smart appearance, there was a devious treachery. He was definitely not to be trusted — which was why Kerra was suspicious of his apparent delight at seeing her here. The rules dictated that bids for the catering contract should all be submitted in strictest confidence, yet she was sure that Murray had been expecting them.

'We have quite a bit of work to do setting this lot up,' Kerra said quickly.

Murray squinted behind her.

'Need any help?'

She mustered her sweetest smile.

'Thanks for the offer, but we'll manage just fine.'

'You know where to come if you need me.'

Kerra didn't miss the smirk in his smile as he turned away with a final flourish of his hand, and called back, 'Let battle commence.'

She watched him retreat and a shiver ran down her spine. It was too easy. Murray Glenn was up to something. She went back to the van and began carrying trays to the trestle tables that had been provided for them. Systematically she went though the carefully packed food. It all looked fine. But something was wrong, she was sure of it.

It was Will who spotted the empty gas cylinder. Two had been put in the van to use as a power supply, enabling them to cook the bacon and burgers for the baps they'd brought, and to provide boiling water for the drinks. Kerra had checked them herself last night and both were full. So how could one now be empty?

'We'll have enough gas in the one cylinder to be going on with, but it certainly won't last the day,' Will said, a worried frown creasing his young brow.

Kerra pressed her lips tightly together and narrowed a stare in Murray's direction.

'Can you two hold the fort while I nip back for a replacement?'

The both nodded, and Will loaded the empty cylinder back onto the van.

'I'll be as quick as I can,' she said, climbing into the driving seat. The flap at the far end of the marquee had been lifted and she saw Murray step out.

'Forgotten something?' he called after her, feigning concern, but he was smiling as she drove off.

There were two possibilities about the empty gas cylinder. Kerra could have made a mistake, and goodness knows her mind hadn't been a hundred percent on this farm job, or the cylinder had been changed, a full one swapped for an empty one. If that was the case then she had no doubt about who was at the bottom of it. But why — and how had he managed it? The man ran a hotel, a much bigger and more financially lucrative business than hers would ever be, yet he felt threatened. It didn't make sense.

She'd made good time getting back to base and quickly swapped the useless cylinder for a full one. She could hear the chink of teacups and buzz of voices coming from the tearoom and put her head round the door. Fiona looked up.

'Is there a problem?'

Kerra gave a quick recap of the morning's little drama and watched Fiona's eyes cloud over.

'How could that happen?' She frowned.

Kerra shrugged and glanced round the busy tables.

'I don't suppose Duncan's been back?'

Fiona shook her head miserably.

'He's hardly likely to do that after what I said to him.'

Kerra reached out and touched her friend's shoulder.

'Try not to worry about it.' She managed a smile. 'I'm sure it will all be fine.' She knew she was giving advice she couldn't follow herself, but what could she do?

She checked her watch. She'd been away less than half an hour. The health centre was closed on a Saturday, but she might just catch Duncan at home.

A few minutes later she was driving past his cottage. Her heart skipped a beat when she spotted his red car in the drive. But there was a big green 4x4 vehicle parked in front of his gate. She wasn't going to barge in if he had a visitor, so she drove past the house, turning up the side, from where she could see the big, grassed back garden. A woman was sitting with her back to her at a rickety wrought-iron table. She stood up as Duncan came towards her, carrying drinks in two tall glasses.

The sun glinted on her mane of copper hair, and the strapless black top and shorts showed off the shapely figure to perfection. It was Lauren King.

Kerra gulped. So Duncan hadn't been sitting at home nursing his wounds after all. He was here with the old love of his life — and, from what Kerra could see, they were renewing their acquaintance.

With a heavy heart she drove back to join the others at the farm sale. She'd have to snap out of this mood or she'd be letting all of them down. The three of them had worked so hard over the past few days, producing the freshest, most tasty banquet that could have graced any table. She wasn't about to put all that in jeopardy just because she'd allowed herself to fall for a man who saw her only as a sister.

Despite her efforts to control her feelings, the rest of the day passed in a haze of misery. She knew Will and Janie were giving her strange looks. Several times, Janie came up to her and asked if she was all right. Kerra had fixed a bright smile and nodded.

'Just a bit stressed out, that's all,' she'd murmured. She was relying on their thoroughly organised preparation to see them through the day, and it did. The event was a huge success and the praise and accolades for her efforts came fast and thick.

'You two have been worth your weight in gold today,' she told them as they packed up. 'You can expect a little extra in your pay next week.' She smiled at the surprised grin that passed between them.

The tearoom was closed by the time they got back to Craigallen, and they were all weary as they unloaded the van. Normally Kerra would have stayed behind in the kitchen, spending some time to update her books, but tonight she was so exhausted that she drove straight home.

It was after ten when the patter of rain on the bedroom window woke her next morning. She lifted back the curtain to reveal the dark, grey morning. It suited her mood.

Breakfast in the Morrison home on a Sunday morning was a relaxed affair, with all of them still in their dressing-gowns reading the newspapers.

After breakfast Kerra took a shower, then pulled on an old sweater, tucked her jeans into her boots, and took herself off for a tramp across the hills.

She returned the nodded greetings of the occasional dog-walkers she met on the way, and was glad she didn't meet anyone she knew. She needed the solitude of this day to get her thoughts together, to make some sense of the whole crazy world. She'd hated Duncan yesterday when she saw him with Lauren. But what had he done? It wasn't his fault if he was in love with her. She knew what it was like to be in love. She'd just picked the wrong man.

She'd tucked her mobile phone into her pocket before leaving the cottage. She'd no idea why she'd done that. No-one was likely to ring her. But its sudden buzzing in her pocket made her start and for a split second she wondered if it might be Duncan calling. When she fished it out of her pocket it was Marcus's name that flashed on the screen.

'How did the farm sale go yesterday?' he demanded with no polite preamble. Kerra frowned. She couldn't remember having mentioned it to him.

'Yes, it went well, Marcus.' She hesitated.

Kerra told him about all the little mishaps leading up to the event, culminating in her theory that the gas bottles had been switched. She waited for him to wade in with an opinion, but Marcus was strangely quiet, then he said, 'So you still have the gremlins, then?'

'It seems that way. Actually it wouldn't have been so bad if Murray Glenn hadn't been there gloating. At least, that's what it looked like to me.'

'He was there, then?'

Kerra nodded into the phone.

'The Crofters' Arms supplied the drinks, but I got the impression that he felt he should have been awarded the catering contract for the food.'

'I shouldn't waste time worrying

about him, pet. Did the punters appreciate your efforts?'

'Actually, yes, they did.'

'As I knew they would,' came the immediate reply. 'I must go now, little one. Keep in touch.'

The rain was still pouring down, but her chat with her old friend had made Kerra feel marginally better. However, her black mood returned as she neared home again. If her parents noticed, they said nothing. Maybe she was learning to hide her feelings a bit better than she realised.

The sun had appeared again when she woke next morning and drew back her bedroom curtains. A blue haze of early morning dew glistened on the grass. In spite of herself, she was actually feeling a bit better. It was going to be a lovely day.

'Meals on wheels?' her father teased as she joined him and her mother at the breakfast table. 'I thought you were supposed to be a ruthless business-woman.'

'I leave that kind of thing to the man at the Crofters' Arms,' Kerra said. 'Besides, it's no trouble to make up a dozen or so meals in a good cause now and again.'

'But you're delivering them as well, remember.' Fraser Morrison reached for another roll and spread it with a thick layer of yellow farm butter. 'Some of these old folks live out in the wilds.'

Kerra gave him a dubious grin.

'Well, in some pretty far-flung places,' he conceded.

Kerra nodded.

'I know, Dad, and it's usually the job of the volunteers, but they're a person down this week, so I offered to help.' She squinted out of the window to the far hills. Yesterday's rain was a memory, and the hills were now bathed in bright early morning sunshine. 'Anyway,' she went on, her mood a lot more cheerful than the one she'd been in the previous day. 'It's not exactly a hardship to drive around the countryside on a morning like this.'

Her father was smiling fondly at her. He knew just how busy his daughter was, but it was typical of her not to turn anyone away if they needed her help. He tilted his head to one side and held out his arms.

'Come here,' he said.

She turned to hug him and his voice was muffled as he spoke softly into her hair.

'I don't say this enough, Kerra, but we're proud of you.'

He turned suddenly, reaching for his cap, which he'd left on a peg at the back of the kitchen door. But Kerra had seen the glint of wetness in her father's eyes as he turned away. She looked round and was surprised to see her mother stuff a scrunched-up hanky back into her apron pocket, the bright traces of tears still in her eyes.

'For heaven's sake, what's wrong with everybody this morning?' Kerra laughed.

They rose early in the Morrison household so it was just eight o'clock when her car pulled into the yard behind the tearoom and kitchen. There was a large order of game pies, vol-au-vents and sandwich fillings to prepare for an event next day at one of the area's many shooting lodges. An extra dozen meals wouldn't cause any problems.

Fiona was first to arrive and, after brief greetings that included no mention of Duncan or Murray Glenn, she went through to prepare for her day in the busy tearoom. Janie turned up on cue at nine, and Will was a few minutes behind her. Kerra set them preparing food for the shooting lodge order.

She dished up generous slices of pie into the silver-coloured meal boxes, and added a crisp salad. Home-made apple pie and custard never went wrong for a pudding, not even in the warmest weather. Satisfied that she'd be doing her diners proud, she stacked the boxes into their containers and loaded them into her car.

Her mother, herself a volunteer for

the organisation during the winter months, had told her how important the visits of the cheery volunteers were to the older people. In this part of the Highlands many pensioners still lived alone in remote crofts, and although they welcomed the meals, they appreciated the company just as much.

With that in mind, Kerra set off just after ten, allowing herself plenty of time to stop for a chat at each house she visited. The first six calls were to folk in Craigallen, and two more customers were just on the outskirts. The next call was a mile out of town, and the last, half a mile away. By the time she found Ben Hughes's low cottage along a narrow rutted lane, it was almost one o'clock.

She parked at the side of the house, glancing towards the tiny windows for any sign of a welcome, but nothing was stirring so she got out of the car. There was no sign of a bell so Kerra knocked on it with her fist.

'Mr Hughes. It's Meals On Wheels,

Ben. I've brought your lunch.' She listened but could hear only the sound of the wind rustling through the tangle of weeds that surrounded the cottage. She was getting an uneasy feeling about this. She hammered the door. 'Ben? Are you there?'

He could, of course, have gone into town shopping, but she'd heard he didn't go out much any more. She crept round the back, opening a gate into what must once have been a vegetable garden.

The back door was ajar and she went in, holding her breath. The room was dark but Kerra could make out a sink. There was no collection of dirty dishes; cups, plates and cutlery had been washed and were stacked on a draining board. Clearly Ben Hughes was attempting to make the best of his situation. She walked on, calling Ben's name, but there was still no response.

She didn't notice the bulky figure on the floor until she almost tripped over him.

'Ben!' Her hand flew to her mouth. For a split second she couldn't move, then her professionalism clicked in. Reaching for her mobile she punched in 999, at the same time touching her fingers to his wrist for any sign of a pulse. It was very faint, but it was there. She flicked the phone to loudspeaker mode, praying she could remember the resuscitation procedure she'd learned as a trainee chef.

'The ambulance is on its way,' the voice at the other end of the phone said, 'but the First Responder will probably get to you first. Keep the line open.'

'Come on, Ben, open your eyes,' she pleaded.

It seemed to take for ever before she heard the crunch of tyres and a vehicle screeching to a stop outside. Suddenly the front door burst open and Duncan was on his knees beside her, yanking open a case that contained a defibrillator.

'Stand back, Kerra. I'll take over

now. You watch for the ambulance. This isn't an easy place to find.'

Kerra got shakily to her feet and went to the door. Across the fields she could see the outline of the speeding ambulance and ran along the lane to wave it in. Loose stones flew in all directions as it came to a dramatic stop behind Duncan's red sports car. Two green-suited paramedics piled out, heaving heavy medical packs onto their backs as they ran.

She heard Duncan's voice as they rushed past her.

'He's breathing,' he called to them. 'But let's not waste time getting him off to hospital.'

Kerra touched the wall for support. Duncan had said he was alive. She felt her bottom lip quiver and was power-less to stop the tears coursing down her cheeks. That's how Duncan found her as they took Ben off to hospital on a stretcher. She felt his arms go round her.

'You saved a man's life today, Kerra,'

he said gently, his fingers caressing her hair. 'I think that's something worth celebrating.'

She looked up and saw the admiration in his grey eyes — or had it been more than that? She wasn't sure, for he was carefully lifting back a strand of pale hair that had fallen over her face. He traced the line of her jaw and, for one heart-stopping moment, she thought he was going to kiss her. But then he drew back so suddenly that she wondered if she had dreamed the moment.

'I think we both deserve a stiff drink after that. What do you say?'

She glanced at their cars.

'I think we'll have to make that a coffee.'

A Note For Fiona

There was a new spring in Kerra's step when she got back to Craigallen. Duncan had found a farm shop and treated her to a cream tea. He'd teased her about checking out the competition, but excellent though the home-baked scones were, the place was so far out of town that it wouldn't affect her place.

It was only when she reached base and stepped back into the catering kitchen that she remembered promising Fiona that she would talk to Duncan on her behalf and try to smooth over the harsh words they had lashed out on each other over Murray Glenn. But thinking back over the past couple of hours, if Duncan had been upset at his sister's words, it obviously hadn't lasted.

The shooting event they were preparing for was still two days away, but Will and Janie had been busy in her absence and most of the advance preparations had been done. She'd settled to dealing with the accounts when her mobile rang.

'Good news,' Matthew West announced. 'The people who were interested in buying Sinclair's premises have confirmed they're going ahead with it. We've sold your business, Kerra. Any chance of you coming up to Inverness in the morning to sign the papers?'

'Try and stop me.' Kerra laughed. 'That's wonderful.'

'Is nine o'clock too early for you?'

'No problem,' Kerra said, still beaming as Fiona came into the kitchen.

'You look like you've just won the lottery,' she said.

'I've sold Uncle Sinclair's shop.' Kerra grinned, her eyes shining.

Fiona clapped her hands and did a little dance before hugging her.

'That's wonderful.' She nodded to the tearoom. 'Duncan's here. He came to apologise. Come through and tell him your news.'

Heart pounding, Kerra followed Fiona into the tearoom. Only two of the tables were occupied. Duncan was standing by the counter and looked up, smiling, as she approached.

'Kerra's had some good news,' Fiona announced, looking back at her friend. 'Go on, tell him.'

Kerra took a deep breath.

'The solicitor has found a buyer for my uncle's business in Inverness,' she said excitedly. 'I'm going through there in the morning to sign the relevant documents.'

'Wow!' Duncan said, throwing his arms around her, 'That's wonderful news.' He heard her gasp and released her, looking a little embarrassed. 'I'm sorry,' he said quietly, examining her face. 'Did I hurt you?'

She could feel her cheeks colouring, but she was too happy to worry about it as just as he'd pulled away she'd seen that same look of tenderness that she'd seen in his eyes earlier, outside Ben

Hughes's cottage.

'Tomorrow's my day off,' he said. 'I could take you through, if you'd like?'

She swallowed, giving him a silent nod.

'I'll take that as a yes.' He grinned.

★   ★   ★

Kerra took a long time in the shower next morning. She so wanted to believe Duncan had made his offer because he wanted to spend time with her. But Kerra had no reason to believe he considered her any more than just a friend. Maybe he wanted to talk over his feelings for Lauren or ask her advice? She prayed this wouldn't be the case.

It was just after eight when they heard his car roll into the yard.

'That'll be the doctor,' Kerra's father said.

Her mother tutted, and gave him a little nudge.

'His name's Duncan,' she said,

grinning at her daughter. Then she added, 'This is a big day for you, Kerra. Just think, by the time you come back tonight, you will be a financially independent woman.'

'I know.' She tried to keep her breathing even. 'I can hardly believe all this is happening.' She hadn't told her parents because she didn't want them to worry, but money had certainly been getting tight. Her overheads — the staff's wages, plus having to lay out cash to buy essential ingredients — were creeping up all the time, and her bank balance was suffering. Not all clients settled up on time, so there was always a cash flow worry. But her mother was right. The settlement of her uncle's business would solve those problems. It also meant money could be released to set up the five trust funds for Sarah's and David's children.

'Not late, am I?' Duncan breezed into the kitchen and smiled at the three faces.

Kerra grabbed her bag.

'Not if you can get me to Matthew West's office by nine.'

The road was busier than either of them had expected at that time of day. An ambulance, blue lights flashing, was approaching at speed from behind them. Duncan pulled into the verge to allow it to pass, and Kerra could see other vehicles ahead doing the same. It reminded her of Ben Hughes and she asked Duncan if there was any news.

'He's not out of the woods. It was a severe heart attack. Another half an hour and it might have been too late.'

Duncan glanced at her and saw her shiver.

'He owes you his life, Kerra,' he said quietly.

As they drove through Inverness, Kerra's thoughts focused on the meeting ahead of her. She was feeling the same surge of uncertainty she'd experienced the first time she'd walked into the solicitor's office. It had only been a few months before, yet it seemed a lifetime ago. Duncan had offered to wait outside while she conducted her business in private, but she asked him to stay with her.

Edward and Valerie Shroot were an Edinburgh couple in their early forties. The man wore rimless spectacles and his greying hair was fringed around his bald patch. Mrs Shroot was small, immaculately dressed in a grey trouser suit, and had intelligent brown eyes that were fixed on Kerra's face.

She extended a hand to each one in turn.

'The workshop is just perfect for me,' Edward Shroot said. 'I'm a tailor, like your uncle, but our Edinburgh premises became too expensive to lease, so I had to let it go.' He scratched his cheek and glanced across at his wife. 'We'd just about given up hope of finding anywhere else.'

Kerra's eyes lit up.

'Does this mean you plan to run a similar business to my uncle's?'

'With a bit of modernising, of course,' Valerie Shroot cut in. 'But we'll be running it much along the same lines.'

Kerra looked across at Matthew West, who was nodding his approval.

'If you could each just sign here.' He smiled, offering his pen. 'Then we'll have a sale.'

They all indulged in another round of handshakes.

'If there's anything I can do to help, please don't hesitate to call me,' Kerra said, handing Edward Shroot one of her business cards, which he passed across to his wife.

He gave a little cough.

'There might be something you could do for us.'

Kerra raised an eyebrow, encouraging him to continue.

'I was wondering . . . ' He hesitated, and Mrs Shroot took over.

'What Edward is trying to say is that we were wondering if your uncle kept a list of his clients? We're having to start fresh here in Inverness, and if you did know of a few potential customers we could contact . . . '

Kerra frowned at the solicitor.

'I'm sure Uncle Sinclair kept a ledger.' She made a shape with her hands. 'I can remember a leather book.'

'It wasn't in the workshop, or the drapery,' he said. 'I was wondering if he took it home with him?'

'Could be,' Kerra said. 'I could ring Sarah. She might know.' She turned to the Shroots. 'Can you leave this with me for a day or so and I'll find out what I can. If the ledger is at Muirend then I see no problem about you having it.'

There were smiles all round as they left, emerging back into the Inverness sunshine.

'I feel like I'm walking on air,' Kerra confided as she skipped beside Duncan through the city centre. 'And now that I'm a woman of means, I can afford to buy you lunch.'

Duncan checked his watch and grinned down at her.

'We are about three hours too early for that. What about a drink?'

'I've a much better idea,' Kerra said, her eyes gleaming. 'If you'd like to indulge me, that is.'

He arched a quizzical eyebrow at her.

'We could drive to Muirend, Uncle Sinclair's old house. It's only a couple of miles the other side of Inverness.'

'But wasn't that left to your cousins?' Kerra nodded.

'It was, but I spent a big chunk of my childhood there. I used to come through during the school holidays to stay with Uncle Sinclair and Aunt Avril. Besides . . . ' She grinned teasingly. 'I have to find that ledger.'

Duncan was following her directions out of Inverness and took the busy road that led to the city's small airport. On her instructions, he took a left turn, driving along the narrow country road for a mile before turning into a lane that ended in high metal gates.

'This is Muirend,' she said with a flourish.

They parked and got out of the car. Duncan peered through the gates at the big granite-built house beyond.

'Impressive,' he said.

'Let's see if we can get in.' Kerra got out of the car and ran towards the gate. They swung open at her push. She looked back, grinning. 'Come on.'

Duncan followed dutifully, walking with her to the back of the house where a large expanse of lawn stretched out before them. The doors to the house were all locked and she made a mental note to ring Sarah, now that they were on better terms, and ask her to look for that ledger and take it to Matthew West's office.

'Oh, look!' Kerra exclaimed. 'The swing's still here.' She ran towards it, but it looked too rusty to be safe. She spun round, taking in the familiar garden. 'I was a fairy princess here, and this was my domain.'

She turned and realised he'd been watching her, with an indulgent smile. She flushed.

'You can laugh,' she said, 'but this place was really important to me.'

He searched her face with serious grey eyes.

'I'm not laughing,' he said quietly.

A sound from the front of the house sent them hurrying to find the cause. A small white van had arrived and was parked by the gates. A man in a white boiler suit was pasting a *Sold* notice across the *For Sale* board so prominently displayed in the front garden. His task completed, he nodded to them and drove away, leaving Kerra and Duncan staring at his handiwork.

'It's really happened. The house has been sold.' She felt the prick of tears and held her hands to her cheeks. 'All those good times, all those memories.' Her voice was a whisper. The tears were flowing unchecked now, and Kerra was powerless to stop them.

All at once she felt Duncan's arms come around her, sensed the warmth of his breath against her cheek. He was cradling her, stroking her hair. Then he tilted up her face and his mouth came down on hers. It was the gentlest whisper of kiss, but it shot a bolt of lightening through Kerra's whole being. She closed her eyes and gave herself up to the delicious moment.

When they broke apart, she thought he would pull away as he had before when he'd got close to her. But this time he slid his arm around her shoulders as they walked slowly back to the car.

'I've got a treat for you.' He grinned, not taking his eyes from the road as the headed back to Inverness. 'Something to really cheer you up again.'

Kerra smiled at his handsome profile. She was too intrigued to tell him she didn't need cheering up. The tears at the house had been one indulgent moment of nostalgia. This was turning out to be one of the happiest days Kerra had ever known.

They crossed the Cromarty Bridge, turning off to head into the Black Isle — which wasn't an island at all, nor was it black. It was one of those quirky bits of Highland reasoning and, although there were many theories, no-one knew for certain why the area was so named.

Hedgerows raced past on either side, and Kerra could see the blue waters of the Moray Firth stretching ahead.

She was still in a daze from that kiss. A couple of times she snatched a glance at Duncan's profile just to make sure she wasn't imagining being here with him.

'Where are we going?' she asked playfully.

'I told you,' he said. 'It's a surprise.' There was smugness about his smile that was intriguing her.

The little red sports car was bowling along a narrow lane, past the greens of a golf course, heading for the shores of the firth. Duncan pulled up alongside a few other parked cars in a clearing facing the water. He spread his arms wide as though displaying the view to the world.

'What do you think?' he asked. 'Isn't it breathtaking?'

Kerra could only nod in agreement.

She'd never been to this spot before and clasped her hands in delight. In the distance she could make out the vaulted framework of the bridge they'd just driven across.

'Come on,' he said, getting out of the car. 'There's more to see.'

He took her hand and helped her to jump down onto the pebbled beach, and they strolled together by the water's edge to the end of the peninsula, where a crowd had gathered. Some people had cameras around their necks, others fiddled with more elaborate photographic equipment. They were all looking out across the firth.

'What are they waiting for?' Kerra frowned.

Duncan was looking particularly pleased with himself. He pointed across the water.

'Just keep looking out there, Kerra. You'll see.'

And she did, and she gasped as three bottlenose dolphins broke the surface of the water to arc in formation. A sigh went up from the crowd and cameras began to whirr. Further out more dolphins were surfacing, each new sighting bringing gasps of excitement from the watchers.

'This is wonderful, Duncan,' she breathed, wide-eyed.

He nodded.

'The dolphins come in with the tide to feed. They might even catch a salmon or two, if they're lucky.'

'How did you find this place?' Kerra murmured, her eyes trained on the waves for the next thrilling appearance.

'I've been here before,' he said quietly.

Kerra looked up at him, wondering if he'd brought Lauren here.

'Why didn't you tell me?' she said, not quite sure what she was asking him.

But he lifted a lock of blonde hair from her face.

'That would have spoiled the surprise,' he said softly.

She reached up and caught his hand.

'It's a wonderful surprise, Duncan,'

she said, her voice no louder than a whisper. 'Thank you.'

He nodded, and she saw him swallow as he turned back, his eyes narrowing as they scanned the waves. If he'd stayed gazing at her for a second longer he would have taken her in his arms. He so much wanted to give in to his feelings, but he couldn't bear the pain of being hurt so deeply again. He had responsibilities now, and his career was his priority.

Dr Grant had returned from leave and had officially announced his retirement. He'd already given his full backing for Duncan to join the practice as his replacement. He had a future in Craigallen — and one day he might even marry, but the relationship would be based on shared interests and being comfortable in each other's company. His heart wouldn't miss a beat every time he saw her, and no bells would ring in his head.

Then there was the business with Marcus. He hadn't liked going behind

Kerra's back, but if anyone could find out about Murray Glenn's background it was him.

The crowd had started to disperse and he jerked his thoughts back to the present. He looked down at Kerra. She was still watching the dolphins. She looked like a child who had just discovered the wonders of the world for the first time. It would have been so easy to step forward and take her in his arms. But instead, he gave himself a mental shake.

'Let's get lunch now,' he said. If she noticed the sudden sharpness in his voice there was no sign of it.

'Good idea,' she said, without looking at him.

They made their way back to the car in silence. Kerra looked back across the firth as they drove away. The dolphins were still performing.

'This is the place,' Duncan said ten minutes later as they approached a pub. Judging by the number of vehicles in its car park, it was a popular place to eat.

'What do you think?' he asked.

'It looks fine.' She nodded.

They found a tiny space at the far end of the car park and Duncan squeezed the car into it. Kerra realised, with a sudden jolt, that she was famished. They found a corner table and quickly made their choices from the menu. A few minutes after going to the bar to order their food, Duncan was back, grim-faced.

'Is something wrong?' Kerra was instantly on her guard.

'That depends on how you look at it.' He nodded across the room. 'You'll never guess who I've just spotted over there, and he's not alone.'

The bar was a horse-shoe shape and Kerra stood up to peer across in the direction Duncan was indicating. The couple had their heads bent low across the table, but there was no mistaking the broad shoulders of Murray Glenn.

She frowned. There was no reason why he shouldn't be having lunch in a country pub — even one as far off the beaten track as this. It was his companion that raised her eyebrows. It was Becky Stuart. Kerra sank back into her seat, her face ashen.

'I know the girl,' she said, her voice flat.

Duncan squinted back across at the couple, waiting for her to go on.

'She's been working in my kitchen for the past week.'

It took a minute for Duncan to register the implication, and then he turned to stare at her.

'Are you suggesting what I think you are?'

Kerra nodded.

'Until now I had only suspected all those unexplained mishaps could have been deliberate, but now I'm certain.' Her eyes narrowed. 'And if I'm right, that little madam over there is responsible.'

'Let me get this straight, you're saying that this Becky person was working under instruction from Glenn to sabotage your business?'

Kerra pursed her lips.

'But that's incredible — even for him,' Duncan said.

'You haven't heard the rest of it yet.'

His stare was grave.

'Go on,' he said.

Kerra related the drama of the empty gas cylinder, and her flight back to Craigallen for a replacement. Reliving the tale brought back the image of Lauren, seductive in her glamorous black sun top and shorts, sharing a drink with Duncan in the intimacy of his garden. She looked away, trying to obliterate the unwanted image from her mind.

'You think Becky switched the cylinders?'

Kerra shrugged.

'All I can say is that Murray was looking very pleased with himself that day, and I know I checked those cylinders when they were loaded onto the van the previous evening. What other explanation could there be?'

The waitress arrived with the steaks

they had ordered, and they ate in silence for the next ten minutes.

'I've been thinking about what you suggested the other day, Kerra.' Duncan pushed his empty plate aside and met her eyes, 'You were worried that Murray was using Fiona to get back at you. It all felt a bit far-fetched then, but now I'm not so sure.

'All those little incidents — if you'd been thinking along the lines that they weren't accidents, then the obvious culprit would be a member of staff.' His eyebrows met in a frown. 'And Fiona was going out with Murray, who just happened to have it in for you.'

'I never suspected Fiona,' Kerra said, her eyes widening. 'But you're right. She would have been the obvious one to blame. I think that's what Murray was depending on.'

She saw the spark of anger glint in his grey eyes and touched his arm.

'You're not thinking of tackling Glenn with any of this, I hope. Remember, we don't have any proof.'

On the periphery of her vision she saw Murray and Becky get up from their table.

'They're leaving,' she hissed. 'They mustn't see us.'

If the couple passed their table, there would be no avoiding them. Then Kerra let out a relieved sigh.

'It's OK,' she said. 'There's another door over there and they're making for that.'

They watched the pair leave, straining to catch a glimpse of them in the car park.

'I think that's his car — the dark Vauxhall over there,' Kerra said. It was the one she'd seen Fiona in not so long ago. By the time Murray and Becky reached it, their arms were entwined around each other. And when they stopped, Murray bent down to kiss his companion on the mouth.

'So, more than just good friends, then,' Duncan said grimly. 'I'd be willing to guess that Fiona doesn't know about this.'

Kerra was in a sombre mood as they drove back to Craigallen. Duncan had agreed to let her break the news to Fiona that the man she was mad about was two-timing her. She wondered how deeply her friend cared for the philandering Murray. Was she in the same situation with Duncan, she wondered? He had kissed her, after all — even though he was seeing Lauren. She had the proof of her own eyes to confirm that.

But that kiss . . . she was remembering the delicious sensation that swept through her when his lips touched hers. Had that been a kiss of comfort from one old friend to another? It would be perfectly natural for a friend to put his arms around you at a time like that. She reached up to rub her forehead. Had she misinterpreted the whole thing?

'Are you all right, Kerra?'

His worried glance brought her back to the present. She would have to be on her guard from now on. If friendship was the most she could expect from Duncan then she would have to accept that. From now on she would keep her overactive imagination in check.

It was mid-afternoon when they arrived back in Craigallen. She was aware that her car was still back at her parents' cottage, but she asked him to drop her off at the tearoom. She would ask Fiona to give her a lift home. It would be a good opportunity to have the chat she was dreading.

'How did things go in Inverness?' Will asked as Kerra walked in.

'Fine,' she said. She knew that he and Janie would be expecting to hear a more detailed account of the morning's events, but right at that moment she lacked the energy to go into it. 'My uncle's business has a new owner,' she said, forcing a smile. She saw the relieved look that shot between them and realised that they had probably been worrying about the security of their jobs.

Fiona was carrying a tray of teas to

the only table occupied. It was a group of three women who were earnestly engaged in what Kerra suspected was serious gossiping. She looked up, her face flushed, and forced a smile. There was no friendly greeting, no enquiry about the sale of the business. She waited until Fiona had served her customers and came back to join her behind the counter.

'Is something wrong, Fiona?' She hardly needed to ask. It was plainly obvious that she was upset.

In an irritated gesture, Fiona swept away a lock of stray hair with the back of her hand, and bit her lip. She reached into her pocket, pulled out a crumpled sheet of paper and handed it to Kerra without a word.

Kerra smoothed it out on the corner, and her brow wrinkled. The words, scrawled in thick, black felt-tipped pen screamed back at her. *Your boyfriend is cheating on you.*

Kerra sank onto the stool behind the counter.

'Oh, Fiona. I'm so sorry.'

Fiona rounded on her, her eyes wide. 'You don't believe that?' She pointed at the note as though it was a poisoned chalice. 'Somebody's got it in for me, and it doesn't take much to guess who that is!'

Kerra frowned.

'You know who's done this?' For that split second she wondered if Fiona actually knew about Becky. But how could she?

'It's Duncan! Who else?' the younger girl raged. 'We both know he wants me to stop seeing Murray. I just never believed he would take things this far.'

The three customers Fiona had just served were glancing over, their heads going down as they digested this conversation.

'We can't discuss this here,' Kerra said. 'I was actually going to ask you for a lift home this evening. I don't have my car.'

'Of course,' Fiona said flatly. 'I'll be closing up when that table leaves.'

In Strictest Confidence

Kerra sat in Fiona's car, not sure where to begin. She couldn't let her go on believing Duncan had written such a vicious thing, but as she glanced at her friend's stony profile, she had an uneasy feeling there was worse to come.

They'd driven out of the town and were now going along the country road, heading for Kerra's home. She took a deep breath. It's now or never, she thought.

'Can you pull in along here for a minute, please, Fiona?'

Her friend slowed the car and steered it into the space in front of a barred gate to a field of black and white cows. A dozen pairs of doleful brown eyes watched them.

Fiona turned with a sigh.

'What's wrong?'

'It's that note. There's no way

Duncan wrote it.'

Fiona raised an eyebrow.

'You know that for sure, do you? Oh, Kerra. It has to have been him. He's made it plain he doesn't want me seeing Murray.'

Kerra bit her lip.

'He has good reason.' She hesitated, choosing her words. 'The note was right. Murray has been seeing somebody else. Duncan and I saw them together earlier.'

Fiona stared at her.

'You're lying.'

Kerra took her hand.

'Just hear me out, Fiona. You know about all the little incidents in the kitchen — the things going missing and then that business of the gas cylinders at the farm sale?' She stopped for a breath. 'I think Murray was behind all that.'

Fiona's eyes widened and she stared at Kerra as though she'd suddenly gone mad.

'But Murray has never been in your

kitchen. How could you think that?'

'Murray might not have been in the kitchen, but his girlfriend has.' Kerra took another deep breath. 'It was Becky. Duncan and I saw them kissing, Fiona.'

Without a word, Fiona turned and restarted the car engine. Five minutes later they had driven into the yard behind her parents' cottage.

'Please come inside for a minute, Fiona. You need to calm down before driving any further.'

But Fiona shook her head.

'Goodnight, Kerra.'

Kerra watched her take off at speed out of the yard and shivered. She shouldn't be driving at all, not in her present mood. But what could she do about it?

'Is that you, Kerra?' her mother called from the kitchen.

Kerra stuck her head round the door.

'I have to go back out, Mum. I shouldn't be too long.'

All she could think of was to tell

Duncan. He would know what to do. But when she arrived at his terraced cottage, instead of stopping, she put her foot on the accelerator and shot past. The big dark 4x4 that she'd seen parked outside his gate once before was there again. Duncan was entertaining Lauren King.

That night she tried to put thoughts of the pair of them out of her mind, but they were stuck. She knew she was being selfish. It was Fiona who deserved her sympathy. She couldn't even be trusted to support her friend when she needed it most.

★ ★ ★

'Don't tell me you're having trouble sleeping as well,' Fiona said, glancing at the wall clock as she came into the kitchen next day and dumped her bag on the floor. 'It's not even eight yet.'

Kerra was perched on a high stool, her business diary open in front of her.

Fiona's eyebrow arched.

'Work? At this time of day?' She frowned. 'And I'm not smelling the coffee. I thought that was the first priority?'

Kerra smiled, pleased that her friend appeared distinctly more cheerful than when she'd driven off last night.

'I was waiting for you to come in and make it,' she quipped back with a tired smile.

Fiona complied, and a few minutes later brought two mugs of steaming coffee to the worktop, before pulling up another stool.

Kerra took a sip.

'I was worried about you, Fiona. Where did you go?'

Fiona stared out across the kitchen.

'I went to find Murray. I couldn't believe what you'd told me.' She shrugged. 'It was like all the people I cared about were suddenly ganging up on me and I didn't deserve that. I had to find out for myself, so I drove to the Crofters' Arms.' Her eyes suddenly narrowed into slits and she said coldly,

'I saw them, Kerra. I saw them kissing, just like you said.'

Kerra's own eyes widened.

'Please don't tell me you tackled them.' Her voice rose in concern.

Fiona shook her head.

'Oh, I'd intended to confront them all right, but I only got as far as the hotel reception. There was no-one on duty at the desk, but I could see through those double glass doors into the bar, and there they were, as brazen as you like.' She bit her lip. 'He was behind the bar; she was perched on one of those plastic stools, looking as though she owned the place. Then he bent across and kissed her on the mouth.' Fiona met Kerra's eyes, and grimaced in disgust. 'I got out of there as fast as I could and drove home.'

Kerra touched her friend's arm.

'I'm so sorry, Fiona,' she said gently. 'You deserved better than that.'

'No, it's fine.' She gave a cough to cover the emotion of reliving the scene. 'I'm grateful to you and Duncan. You

247

both tried to warn me and I wouldn't listen. At least I didn't hang on long enough for them to make a fool out of me.'

She glanced up.

'I suppose Duncan knows you told me?'

'Well, not yet. I did drive over to his place after you left, but he had a visitor. I didn't want to intrude.'

Fiona was frowning at her.

'Not Lauren King?' she asked accusingly.

Kerra swallowed the lump in her throat and nodded.

'It was her car at his gate.'

Fiona slapped the worktop and Kerra started.

'What is wrong with my brother?' She made every word sound like a sentence on its own. 'Hasn't that woman done enough damage?' She shot Kerra an angry glance. 'Her marriage is on the rocks, and they're saying in the village that her husband won't even come for a visit.' She stopped for breath. 'I knew she would try to get back with Duncan. That's what this whole business of coming back to Blairdhu is all about. I just didn't believe that he would fall for it all again.'

She looked up quickly.

'You're sure it was Lauren's car?'

Kerra nodded miserably, her efforts to stop the tremble in her bottom lip failing.

Fiona stared at her. Her friend's feelings for her brother suddenly dawning on her.

'Oh, Kerra. Why didn't you tell me? You're in love with Duncan. I should have guessed.'

Kerra felt the first prick of tears and made an angry swipe at them. She opened her mouth to deny the charge, but it was useless, so she sniffed and said nothing.

'What an idiot I am.' Fiona slapped her palm to her brow. 'You two are perfect for each other.'

'You won't tell Duncan any of this?'

Kerra said quickly, the thought suddenly horrifying her.

Fiona sighed, and gave her a reassuring smile.

'I won't, but I think you should.'

'There's a message for you,' Janie announced to Kerra later that afternoon. She looked round from the sink where she was chopping vegetables. 'It's that Mrs King. I think she wants you to call over there.'

Kerra's heart stopped. The woman who had given her a sleepless night was snapping her fingers and she was supposed to drop everything and drive over there. She didn't think so.

'She said something about a function,' Janie added.

'Function?' Kerra repeated.

'You know, one of these events she runs over at Blairdhu House.'

Kerra shook her head with a resigned smile. She was getting things out of proportion, letting her heart rule her head. She had a business to run. Why wouldn't Lauren King want to hire her again? Her team had done a good job last time, and Lauren had said at the time that she was trying to line up some similar events. She wasn't about to turn work down because she had a bee in her bonnet about the woman's friendship with Duncan.

The big house looked deserted when she drove up the curving drive. This time she parked at the front, climbing the wide steps to the double doors between flanking fluted stone pillars. She thought of the rotting window frames and peeling doors round the back. At least the front of the building had been kept in reasonable order.

She rang the bell and waited for the door to be opened by Heidi. She gave Kerra a friendly smile.

'Mrs King is in the library,' she said. 'I'll show you through.'

Kerra followed, the click of her heels on the stone floors echoing around the high-ceilinged entrance hall.

Lauren was behind a big antique oak desk, a laptop computer open in front of her. She looked up as Kerra walked in and came forward, smiling.

'You can bring the tea in now, Heidi,' she instructed, indicating the big squashy leather chair. Kerra sat down, noting her hostess's smart, business-like cream silk blouse and linen skirt, and wondered if the choice of attire had been for her benefit. She smoothed down her own cotton, floral skirt and refused to feel guilty that she hadn't dressed more formally.

Lauren wasted no time on a preamble.

'Thank you for coming so quickly, Ms Morrison,' she said, taking the chair opposite. 'I think I mentioned to you that I was planning to organise more of these corporate weekends?'

Kerra nodded.

'Well, there are one or two more in the diary now. If we can agree a price then I would like to hire your services again.' She glanced briefly up at her. 'On the same basis as before.'

Kerra remembered she had offered

Blairdhu House a special price for the initial function, on the grounds that it might lead to future orders. She did a mental calculation. If she agreed to the same price she could just about squeeze out a small profit. She'd have to consider this.

She looked up to find Lauren's cool, assessing gaze on her. Kerra was beginning to get an uncomfortable feeling. Was there another purpose behind this invitation? She began to wonder if she'd been right even considering having anything more to do with Lauren King — especially if she was in a relationship with Duncan.

She'd been in two minds about coming to this meeting in the first place, but had convinced herself that it was business. If she were being honest, she was here because her curiosity had got the better of her. But now that she was, she had a unique opportunity to study the woman who had jilted Duncan, and if Fiona was right, had left him with a broken heart. She was determined to make the most of it.

Heidi brought in the tea tray and put it down on the low table between them. Lauren began filling the cups and passed one to Kerra.

'Well?' she asked, arching an elegant eyebrow. 'Do we have a deal?'

Kerra gave her a professional smile.

'I'll have to go back and work out costings, but I should be able to get back to you by tomorrow.'

Lauren pursed her lips, considering.

'Cautious,' she said with a smile that didn't reach her eyes. 'I like that in a businesswoman. Are you local to this area, Ms Morrison?'

Kerra was here to find out about Lauren, not to tell the woman her life story.

'I used to be,' she said dismissively, taking a sip of her tea and returning the delicate cup to its saucer. 'I understand that you have a local connection yourself.'

Lauren looked up quickly, frowning slightly, then her face relaxed into an interested smile.

'You have done your homework, Ms Morrison — or can I call you, Kerra?'

Kerra inclined her head, returning the smile.

'Please do,' she said.

Lauren's green eyes narrowed as she stared at some place deep in the past.

'I should never have left here,' she said, so quietly that Kerra had to strain her ears to catch the words. 'I was happy here once.' She was smiling wistfully. 'A long time ago.'

There was a moment's silence, and then Kerra asked quietly, 'Is that why you and your husband bought this place?'

The mention of her husband snapped Lauren back to the present, as Kerra knew it would.

'My husband indulged me,' Lauren said coldly. 'This was supposed to be our new home, our new life, but I'm afraid Gerald doesn't share my love of Blairdhu.

'He's flown up from London a

couple of times.' She gave Kerra a grim smile. 'At least he's made the effort to get to know the place, but I'm afraid it's all a bit too quiet for him up here. He prefers the London bustle. He's a city boy, you see, and it seems nothing is going to change that.'

If Lauren already knew that then why, Kerra found herself wondering, had she persuaded him to buy Blairdhu House?

'No-one knows about this yet.' She shot Kerra a conspiratorial look. 'But I feel I can trust you, Kerra. The fact is, Gerald and I are divorcing.'

Kerra froze. So this was it. This was the real reason Lauren King had come back to the Scottish Highlands. She was here to get rid of one husband, and find another. It wasn't difficult to see where this was heading. Why else would she and Duncan have been sharing an intimate drink in his garden that day? But more importantly, if Duncan really did regard Kerra as a friend, then why hadn't he mentioned it?

'I don't need to say that what I've just told you is in strictest confidence.' She raised her eyebrow, making Kerra wonder exactly why she had told her. Surely she knew how fast local gossip spread.

Kerra drained her cup. In for a penny, in for a pound.

'Does this mean you'll be selling Blairdhu House, Mrs King?' she asked innocently.

Lauren gave her a warning stare, and then threw her head back, laughing.

'Sell Blairdhu House? I won't be doing that.' Her eyes glittered menacingly. 'I'm here to stay. I told you, Kerra, this is where my roots are. I intend to bring my happy times back.'

Kerra could feel her heart sinking. The woman was talking about Duncan. She got up, her legs shaking, and reached for her bag.

'Thank you for the tea,' she said, struggling to keep her voice level. The interview was concluded with a brief handshake.

Kerra tried to smile, but it froze on her lips.

'I'll let you have all the estimates by the morning,' she said stiffly, wondering why they were keeping up this pretence of a business meeting.

She had the impression of Lauren walking ahead of her, showing her to the door, of getting into her car and driving away from Blairdhu House. If she'd come to discover Lauren King's intentions concerning Duncan, she'd been left in no doubt. The woman was determined to get him back — and there was nothing Kerra could do about it!

Mrs Glenn

Kerra sat for a few minutes considering the conversation the two of them had had, and wondered exactly why she had been invited to Blairdhu House. There had been an undertone to Lauren's revelation about an impending divorce. There had been no mention of Duncan, yet Kerra was sure the woman had been warning her off.

Well, let them play their games, she thought angrily. She'd worked hard to get her new business off the ground, and now people were depending on her to make a success of it. Concentrating on that was the important thing now. What Lauren and Duncan got up to was not her concern, and she didn't plan to waste any more thinking time on it.

She restarted the car's engine and drove back to town.

It was late afternoon when Kerra pulled into the yard behind the tearoom. Will and Janie were still busy in the kitchen and their heads came up as she walked in. She'd advertised a new sandwich delivery service for local businesses and the response had been encouraging. She'd left them preparing the selection of fillings for the next day's deliveries.

Janie was elbow-deep in suds, washing the chef's knives they had been using. Kerra rolled up her sleeves.

'I'll take over here, Janie. You two have done enough work for the day.'

They were pulling on their jackets when they heard her cry of pain. Will's head jerked round.

'Kerra! What have you done?' The water she had been using to clean the knives had turned bright red.

'I think I've cut myself,' she said sheepishly, drawing her hand out of the foam, an ugly red wound slashed across her finger.

Will held up her hand, instructing

Janie to fetch the first-aid box.

'Ask Fiona to come through. This cut needs a stitch.'

Fiona burst in, and with a horrified expression, stared at what was now a spreading pool of blood on the worktop. Will was frantically rummaging through the first-aid box, and as best he could bandaged up the injured finger.

'I'm taking you to the surgery,' Fiona announced, flicking a glance at the clock. 'Duncan should be there.'

Fiona waved away her protests.

'We'll let him be the judge.'

So Kerra, still protesting, was ushered out of the kitchen and into Fiona's car.

The health centre lights were still on when they arrived and Duncan's car was in the staff area.

Eileen Faulds was tidying up her reception area and their appearance brought an irritated frown.

'The surgery's closed,' she said in a weary voice.

261

'We need to see Doctor Crombie,' Fiona insisted. 'Tell him his sister's here.'

Eileen's head jerked up and her eyes widened when she saw Kerra's bandaged hand.

'You might have caught him.'

'Caught who?' Duncan said, walking into the waiting-room. His amused expression quickly turning to concern.

'Come through to my room,' he said, his expression serious. 'Heavens, Kerra! What have you been doing to yourself?' His arm was around her and he was guiding her along the short corridor into his consulting room.

'I'll leave you in Duncan's capable hands,' Fiona called after them. But neither of them heard. A slow smile began to spread across her face. Maybe the day wasn't turning out too badly after all.

'I can't believe everybody's making such a fuss,' Kerra said, trying not to think about the fact that Duncan was holding her hand as he examined the wound.

'It's a bit more than a scratch. You'll need a couple of stitches.' He glanced up at her, smiling. 'I can do it here, if you trust me. It's a simple enough job that will take me no more than a few minutes.'

She was thankful he didn't ask how she'd come by her injury. No chef worth his salt would carelessly submerge his hands in a sink full of razor sharp knives. The fact that her mind had been distracted at the time by thoughts of Lauren was no excuse.

But Duncan hadn't enquired. He'd merely stitched the gaping wound, giving her a sympathetic smile when she winced as he worked. When he'd finished, he stood up, turning to dispose of the soiled bandages and washing his hands in a tiny stainless steel sink.

Still with his back to her, he said, 'I'm glad I've seen you, actually, Kerra. Fiona rang me earlier — '

Kerra's heart was thumping. Surely his sister hadn't gone back on her promise not to mention her feelings?

'She mentioned that you'd told her about Murray and his girlfriend. I'm sorry, Kerra, I shouldn't have left you to do it for me.'

'It was fine,' Kerra said, relief flooding through her. 'Fiona was very upset at first, but I think she knows now what a lucky escape she's had.'

Duncan nodded, turning to meet her eyes.

'That pair shouldn't be allowed to get away with it.'

'You're right,' she agreed resignedly. 'But I'll settle for the whole unpleasant business just stopping now. I don't think Mr Glenn can do me any more harm.'

She didn't see Duncan's eyes narrowing.

'I think we should get you home,' he said.

Rosemary Morrison's eyes went straight to her daughter's hand.

'You've had an accident!' she accused, her eyes widening as she hurried to meet them coming through the back door.

'Oh, don't you start, Mum.' Kerra laughed. 'I'm feeling enough of a fraud as it is.'

'Walking wounded,' Duncan assured with a grin. 'I think your daughter will live.'

'Right.' Rosemary frowned, looking from one to the other, wondering what the joke was. 'Am I allowed to ask how it happened?'

'I cut my finger on a kitchen knife,' Kerra muttered, 'and I'm feeling very embarrassed so can we forget it?'

'If you say so, dear,' Rosemary said uncertainly. Then she turned to Duncan. 'You will stay for supper, won't you? It's only chicken casserole, but there's plenty.'

Kerra held her breath, but when she glanced in his direction he was already heading for the door.

'You're leaving?' Kerra bit her lip at her mother's look of disappointment.

'Don't embarrass him, Mum,' she warned. 'I'm sure he has plenty of other things to do tonight.' She shot him a look of apology, hoping it was masking her own disappointment. Of course he had things to do, she thought bitterly. He would be meeting Lauren King. Maybe that's what had put that extra sparkle in his eyes tonight.

But to her amazement, he turned and said, 'That's very kind of you, Mrs Morrison. I have one or two things to attend to right now, but I could be back within the hour, if that's all right with you.'

Both women were staring at him.

'I'm sorry,' Duncan said, addressing her mother. 'Had you planned to eat earlier than that?'

Rosemary shook her head. A delighted grin had appeared on her face. She glanced to the window, where she could see Fraser, still working in the far field.

'An hour from now will be just fine, Duncan. Kerra's father should be in by then, so we can all eat together.'

Somewhere deep inside her, Kerra could feel her spirits beginning to soar.

She couldn't believe he'd accepted her mother's invitation. She realised he was watching her and she smiled back, not trusting herself to speak.

'See you both later, then.' He grinned and was gone.

Duncan didn't go home to his cottage, but headed instead for the surgery. He'd already begun checking the internet, as Marcus had suggested, and although he hated doing all this research behind Kerra's back, he didn't want to raise her hopes if his search proved negative. He let himself into the building, nodding a greeting to the two cleaners as he went into his room. He used his mobile to click on Marcus's number.

'It's Duncan,' he said. 'How are you, Marcus?'

'Perfection,' the reply came back. He could almost hear Marcus kissing the tips of his fingers.

'Have you any more news for me?'

'Of course,' the bistro owner chirped back. 'When my mind is made up about

267

something, I waste no time. And my mind is made up about your Mr Glenn.'

Duncan felt his pulse quicken.

'What have you found out. Marcus?'

'Well, for a start,' the reply came, 'I've discovered that the man who runs the Crofters' Arms in Craigallen isn't Murray Glenn!'

Duncan's mouth went dry as he sank back in his chair.

'I don't understand. If he's not Glenn, then who is he?'

'His name is Simon Kent. A bit of a playboy, by all accounts.'

Duncan's eyes rolled to the ceiling.

'Now why doesn't that surprise me? But wait a minute, how can he hold a drinks' licence under a pseudonym. I've seen the name above the door.'

'Well spotted, my friend,' Marcus said. 'But Simon Kent doesn't hold the licence. His wife does.'

Duncan gave a low whistle.

'Now, that I wasn't expecting.'

'Me neither, to be honest,' Marcus

came back. 'But it's complicated. Let me explain.'

Duncan listened in disbelief as Marcus told his story.

'I was suspicious of the man from the start,' he said. 'He was going through the motions of being a hotelier, but when you got down to it he didn't know the first thing about the business. He was ignoring the basic principle, which is to keep the customer happy.' He paused. 'Didn't you ask yourself why the place was always empty?'

'Yes, I did wonder about that. Kerra heard he'd told the locals they needn't bother trying to get into the bar because they wouldn't be welcome. He seemed to think he could magic some new, high-class customers out of thin air.'

'Exactly. That is what set my warning bells ringing in the first place. If you remember, I was staying at the Crofters' Arms the night Kerra's tearoom was vandalised. When I got back there I went to the bar for a nightcap. Glenn had sent the staff home and served me himself. He didn't ask about the tearoom, and I didn't mention it, but he seemed very edgy. I got wondering if he'd been involved in causing that damage, so I started to check up on him.'

Marcus gave a little cough.

'I have many good friends in the catering industry, and when they told me that the real Murray Glenn, who ran a string of café bars in the Aberdeen area, had died of a heart attack eighteen months previously, I had to know more.'

'Go on,' Duncan said grimly.

'Well, Simon Kent worked for Glenn. He managed one of his café bars. Anyway, he'd been carrying on an affair with Glenn's wife. I imagine she became even more desirable to him when she was a rich widow.'

Duncan sighed.

'So he married money. But why change his name?'

'My informants tell me that was Mrs

Glenn's idea. Apparently her husband was very popular, and the Glenn name was like a brand of quality in the leisure industry. She didn't want to lose that by becoming Mrs Simon Kent. So, when they married about a year ago, she kept her own name. And Kent, following her logic, changed his name accordingly.'

Duncan frowned.

'But there's no sign of a wife at the Crofters' Arms.'

'She is still based in Aberdeen, and runs the original side of the business. My information is that when the Craigallen hotel came on the market he persuaded Mrs Glenn to buy it, and put him in charge as its manager.'

'But he tells everybody that he owns the place.'

'Perhaps he does. Maybe Mrs Glenn is a generous woman and she saw it as a way of keeping her new husband happy.'

Duncan slumped back in his seat.

'So he's not involved in anything illegal, then?'

'I don't think trashing someone else's business is lawful.'

'But we have no proof that Murray Glenn was behind that,' Duncan reasoned.

'Maybe not, but I would be surprised if he wasn't. I was thinking it might be an idea to drop a hint or two that you know about his past. Something tells me that if you do then Kerra and Fiona would have no more trouble from the man.'

'On second thoughts,' Marcus said, and Duncan could hear the smile in his voice. 'Why don't you leave that little pleasure to me? It's a while since I've been up in Craigallen. I think I'm due another little visit.'

Duncan Explains

Kerra's eyes strayed to the window. He'd said he'd be an hour, so her heart gave a jolt when he turned into the yard early. Her father answered his knock, and his eyes lit up when he saw the bottle of wine Duncan was carrying.

'Now this will go down a treat.' Fraser smiled, accepting the gift and placing it in the centre of the table.

Kerra, suddenly feeling ridiculously shy, turned to lift glasses down from a cupboard.

'Here, let me help.' Duncan's voice was soft in her ear, and she could feel his closeness as he stretched past her to select four stemmed glasses.

They shared companionable small talk as they ate, and when they'd all had their fill, Kerra rose to clear the table. Rosemary moved to help her, but Fraser placed a warning hand on her own, nodding at Duncan, who was already on his feet and taking the dishes from her.

'I think this is my job tonight.' He grinned down at her.

'There's really no need for you to do that,' Rosemary called from the table.

But Duncan had already filled the sink with hot water and was lowering the plates into it. Five minutes later he'd rejoined them. A fresh bottle of wine had appeared and Fraser was refilling the glasses.

Rosemary produced a glass dish filled with fresh fruit salad and a jug of cream and, giving each of them a bowl, invited them to help themselves.

Duncan looked at his replenished glass.

'I still have to drive home,' he reminded them. 'But on the other hand, the rest of you might need a drink when you hear what I have to tell you.'

Kerra and her parents shared a wary look.

'What's that?' she said, not sure she wanted to hear this.

'It's something Marcus has found out about Murray Glenn.' He looked round the table, taking in each surprised face, and laughed. 'Don't worry. It's not bad news.'

Kerra and her parents listened in disbelief as Duncan retold his conversation with Marcus. When he'd finished there was a stunned silence. Then Fraser looked up.

'The man is married and keeping it a secret?' His hands went up in a gesture that indicated he was mystified. 'Why would he do that?'

Duncan shrugged.

'They have a strange marriage. It's not exactly normal for a man to take the name of his wife, but according to Marcus, that's exactly what Murray Glenn did. Mrs Glenn was a widow and insisted on keeping her late husband's name. Marcus understands that she saw it as an important asset to their leisure business.' He put up his hands. 'I guess

Glenn just wanted to latch on to that success.'

'So what is his real name?' Kerra asked.

'Simon Kent,' Duncan said.

Kerra put her fingers to her temple, then remembered her injured one and winced.

'So where was the wife when her husband was busy romancing Fiona and young Becky?'

Rosemary and Fraser had known nothing of this and exchanged shocked expressions.

'Well, according to Marcus, he's got form for this kind of behaviour, which I think his wife, Moira, is aware of.'

'So where is the wife now? Why has she never appeared up here?' Fraser asked.

'She makes infrequent visits, apparently, just to check on her investment.' Duncan looked up. 'Moira Glenn is the real owner of the Crofters' Arms. Did I mention that?'

Three heads shook in unison.

'I haven't seen the books, but given the place is empty most of the time, I can't imagine they show a profit,' Kerra said. 'And why hasn't Marcus told me any of this?' Kerra's blue eyes were now dark with annoyance.

'He didn't want to say anything about it until he had some facts.' Duncan gave her a placating smile. 'I know he feels guilty about that, which is why he's coming up tomorrow to tell you in person.' He didn't mention Marcus's intention to confront the man.

Kerra glanced to the window, where she could see the sun was beginning to set, tingeing the evening clouds pink.

'I need some air,' she said, and in one quick movement headed for the door.

Duncan jumped up and, with an apologetic glance to Rosemary and Fraser, hurried after her. He caught up with her at the gate.

'I'll walk with you,' he offered. 'Marcus really did have your interests at heart. He was suspicious of Glenn from the start, and when the tearoom got trashed . . . ' He let out a sharp breath. 'Well, he was just determined to get to the bottom of it.'

She turned to him, still not sure why she was so angry.

'But there's still no proof that Murray did it.'

'But don't you see?' he reasoned. 'Once he knows we're on to him, he won't try any more little tricks.'

'And who's going to tell him?'

Duncan winced.

'Marcus mentioned that he might.'

Kerra shook her head, but the anger was gone.

'The man's impossible.' She looked up at him with a helpless grin. 'And I don't mean Murray.'

Suddenly they were laughing, and in each other's arms. But what about Lauren? She had to know.

'Let's walk,' she said quickly, stepping away from him.

They strolled side by side. He grinned down at her, sending a tingling sensation down her spine. He picked up a piece of fallen branch, thrashing out at the grass verge as they walked. Why didn't he just come out with it? Was he waiting for her to bring up the subject?

She took a deep breath.

'I was invited to Blairdhu House today,' she said. She saw his jaw tense. 'Lauren asked to see me.'

'How was she?'

Kerra frowned. What did he mean, how was she? She wanted to say the woman had been fishing for information about their friendship, but instead she said, 'She's fine. Why do you ask?'

She waited, trying to steady the thump of her heart.

Duncan took her hand, guiding her to a stone stile by a fence at the side of the road.

'Let's sit for a minute,' he said, his voice low.

They sat in silence, watching the sky turn scarlet. But right at that moment it was casting no magic on Kerra. She waited, dreading his next words.

Duncan cleared his throat, wondering where to start.

'I want to tell you about Lauren,' he said quietly.

Kerra frowned. He was trying to break the news gently to her. She lifted her undamaged hand.

'I already know what you're going to say, Duncan, and it's fine. I know about you and Lauren.'

'Ah, I see Fiona's told you.' He sighed. 'I did rather lose my head, but it didn't take me long to get over it.'

Kerra's head shot up and she stared at him.

'But you're in love with her!'

Duncan's mouth fell open.

'She told you that? I don't believe the woman.'

Kerra put her hand to her head.

'You mean you don't love her?'

'I certainly don't. But I can't seem to get that fact across to her. That's what I wanted to ask your advice about.'

Kerra's heart was pounding so violently that he surely must be able to hear it, and all the time a voice inside her was singing. Duncan didn't love Lauren!

He took her hand.

'It's you that I love, Kerra. I thought you knew that.'

She swallowed, not daring to drag her eyes from his face for fear that he would disappear and she would discover this was all a dream.

He was still talking.

'I didn't tell you because I thought it might scare you off. I know you only want us to be friends, but I can't hide my feelings any longer.'

'Duncan,' she whispered. 'Oh, Duncan. I've waited so long to hear you say that.' Her fingers traced the line of his jaw and she saw the lump in his throat move as he swallowed. Then, with exquisite tenderness, his lips brushed her cheeks, her eyes, her mouth, as he murmured her name. The kiss, when it came, was of such passion that it left them both breathless. His voice was full of emotion when he pulled away.

It was dusk as they strolled, arms entwined, back to the cottage.

'What made you think I was still interested in Lauren?' he asked softly.

'I saw the two of you in your garden. You were having drinks in tall glasses . . .' Her words trailed off. The image still had the power to hurt her.

'Ah,' he said. 'She turned up enquiring after the woman who was injured that day at Blairdhu, and before I knew it she was inside the cottage and heading for the garden. She asked for a drink and by the time I got back she had peeled off her shirt and was wearing this strapless thing.'

'I know. I saw the two of you as I drove away.'

'Did you notice that I was panicking. I don't know what Lauren had in mind, but I wanted her out of there. If you'd driven past a few minutes later you would have seen me bundling her out of the door.'

Kerra tightened her grip around

Duncan's waist and dropped her head onto his shoulder.

'Isn't this the most beautiful sunset you've ever seen? she said dreamily.

He stopped and tilted her chin so she was looking into his eyes.

'There will be lots of sunsets for us now, and lots of sunrises. We have the whole of our lives to enjoy them.'

She gazed up at him, enjoying the feel of the emotions that were surging through her.

'There is only problem,' he said, his eyes twinkling dangerously. 'I was thinking of our wedding reception.'

She arched an eyebrow.

'Do we know any good caterers?'

THE END

We do hope that you have enjoyed reading this large print book.

Did you know that all of our titles are available for purchase?

We publish a wide range of high quality large print books including:
Romances, Mysteries, Classics
General Fiction
Non Fiction and Westerns

Special interest titles available in large print are:
The Little Oxford Dictionary
Music Book, Song Book
Hymn Book, Service Book

Also available from us courtesy of Oxford University Press:
Young Readers' Dictionary
(large print edition)
Young Readers' Thesaurus
(large print edition)

For further information or a free brochure, please contact us at:
Ulverscroft Large Print Books Ltd.,
The Green, Bradgate Road, Anstey,
Leicester, LE7 7FU, England.
Tel: (00 44) **0116 236 4325**
Fax: (00 44) **0116 234 0205**

SEEK NEW HORIZONS

Teresa Ashby

Sister Dominique, already having serious doubts about her calling, is sent on a mercy mission to South America after a devastating earthquake. There, she meets Dr Steve Daniels, and feelings she had never expected to experience again are stirred up. As she is thrown into caring for a relentless stream of casualties, her thoughts are in turmoil. How will she cope in the outside world if she leaves the sisterhood? And dare she allow herself to fall in love again?

HOUSE OF FEAR

Phyllis Mallett

Jill's twenty-first birthday is more than just a milestone — it marks the day her life changes forever . . . A letter arrives on the morning of her birthday; an invitation to travel to Crag House on the remote Scottish island of Inver to stay with the grandfather whose existence she had been completely unaware of. Whilst there, she meets her cousins, Owen and George, and handsome neighbour Robert Cameron. But her visit has involved her in a web of deceit that may threaten her life . . .

SUSPICIOUS HEART

Susan Udy

When Erin discovers that her mother's home and livelihood is under threat from the disturbingly handsome Sebastian, she knows she has to fight his plans every step of the way. However, she quickly realises Sebastian is equally determined to win, and he apparently has the backing of the entire village. When a campaign of intimidation is begun against Erin and her mother, it doesn't take her long to work out that it can only be Sebastian behind it . . .

THE RUNAWAYS

Patricia Robins

When Judith and Rocky elope to Gretna Green they sincerely believe marriage will solve all their problems. But the elopement proves to be the beginning of an entirely new set of difficulties . . . Rocky begins to wonder if his parents were right — is he even in love? Were they too young after all? And in the background Gavin, Judith's boss, watches her disillusionment with a concern which is growing into something more . . .

ANGEL'S TEARS

Teresa Ashby

Born in the same year that the Titanic
sank, seventeen-year-old Cassandra
Grant has the world at her feet. But
tragedy strikes her family and Cassie
has to grow up fast. She falls in love
with Dr Michael Ryan — but then
discovers he is about to be engaged
to be married. Cassie leaves town to
begin training as a midwife and tries
to forget Michael, but tragedy strikes
again and she has to return home
where there are more surprises in
store . . .

DEADLY INHERITANCE

Phyllis Mallett

1927: Sarah Morton is looking forward to starting her new job as a tutor with a wealthy Yorkshire family, but she is taken aback when her young charge, Justin Howard, claims that someone wants him dead — and his great-grandfather seems to believe the same. Could greed be a motivating factor in the attempts to see off the young heir? And is Justin's handsome Uncle Adam really to be trusted?